"Stella..." [...] mind if I..."

His words trailed off like a gust of wind and, as she made no attempt to stop him, he tilted his face ever so slightly and planted a nice kiss on her soft lips. Tasting the wine, he was more than happy to keep it going, which she seemed just as agreeable to.

When Stella pulled away, touching her mouth, she eyed him, ill at ease, and asked tentatively, "What are we doing, Declan? Is this some sort of trip down memory lane for old times' sake? Or what?"

It was a good question and he believed she deserved an answer that they both could live with. Holding her shoulders, Declan answered equably, "The memories of us together were great, by and large, Stella. But I don't see this as some sort of rekindling of yesteryear, per se. Instead, I prefer to view it as creating new memories and whatever they entail moving ahead..."

She held his gaze. "I like that."

"Stella," Declan touched her dainty chin. "You mean it."

HUNTING A PREDATOR

R. BARRI FLOWERS

Harlequin
INTRIGUE

If you purchased this book without a cover you should be aware that this book is stolen property. It was reported as "unsold and destroyed" to the publisher, and neither the author nor the publisher has received any payment for this "stripped book."

In loving memory of my cherished mother, Marjah Aljean, a devoted lifelong fan of Harlequin romance and romantic suspense novels, who inspired me to excel in my personal and professional lives. To H. Loraine (Sleeping Beauty), the true and dearest love of my life and very best friend, whose support has been unwavering through the many terrific years together; as well as the many loyal fans of my romance, suspense, mystery and thriller fiction published over the years. A special shout-out goes to a wonderful group of talents whom I have long admired: Carol, Charmian, Hedy, Krista, Lisa, Peggy, Olivia and Sharon. And last but not least, a nod to my great Harlequin editors, Emma Cole and Denise Zaza, for the wonderful opportunity to lend my literary voice and creative spirit to the Intrigue line, as well as Miranda Indrigo, the wonderful concierge, who serendipitously led me to success with Harlequin Intrigue.

Harlequin
INTRIGUE

MIX
Paper | Supporting responsible forestry
FSC® C021394

Recycling programs for this product may not exist in your area.

ISBN-13: 978-1-335-69032-6

Hunting a Predator

Copyright © 2025 by R. Barri Flowers

All rights reserved. No part of this book may be used or reproduced in any manner whatsoever without written permission.

Without limiting the author's and publisher's exclusive rights, any unauthorized use of this publication to train generative artificial intelligence (AI) technologies is expressly prohibited.

This is a work of fiction. Names, characters, places and incidents are either the product of the author's imagination or are used fictitiously. Any resemblance to actual persons, living or dead, businesses, companies, events or locales is entirely coincidental.

For questions and comments about the quality of this book, please contact us at CustomerService@Harlequin.com.

TM and ® are trademarks of Harlequin Enterprises ULC.

Harlequin Enterprises ULC
22 Adelaide St. West, 41st Floor
Toronto, Ontario M5H 4E3, Canada
www.Harlequin.com

HarperCollins Publishers
Macken House, 39/40 Mayor Street Upper,
Dublin 1, D01 C9W8, Ireland
www.HarperCollins.com

Printed in Lithuania

R. Barri Flowers is an award-winning author of crime, thriller, mystery and romance fiction featuring three-dimensional protagonists, riveting plots, unexpected twists and turns, and heart-pounding climaxes. With an expertise in true crime, serial killers and characterizing dangerous offenders, he is perfectly suited for the Harlequin Intrigue line. Chemistry and conflict between the hero and heroine, attention to detail and incorporating the very latest advances in criminal investigations are the cornerstones of his romantic suspense fiction. Discover more on popular social networks and Wikipedia.

Books by R. Barri Flowers

Harlequin Intrigue

Bureaus of Investigation Mysteries

Killer in Shellview County
Hiding in Alaska
Christmas Bank Heists
Hunting a Predator

The Lynleys of Law Enforcement

Special Agent Witness
Christmas Lights Killer
Murder in the Blue Ridge Mountains
Cold Murder in Kolton Lake
Campus Killer
Mississippi Manhunt

Hawaii CI

The Big Island Killer
Captured on Kauai
Honolulu Cold Homicide

Visit the Author Profile page at Harlequin.com.

CAST OF CHARACTERS

Declan Delgado — A special agent with the Kansas Bureau of Investigation who is in pursuit of a serial killer in the town of Bends Lake, Kansas. A widower, he recruits his late wife's sister, a criminal profiler, who Declan was once involved with, to help solve the case. Can they rekindle the passions they once shared?

Stella Bailey — An FBI behavioral analyst who returns to her hometown to assist in a serial killer case. Working with an ex-boyfriend, with whom she has a complicated history, proves to be challenging, while stirring up old feelings that are brought to the surface.

Ursula Liebert — A KBI special agent who is dedicated to bringing the cold-blooded killer to justice, whatever the price.

Gayle Reese — A high school classmate of Stella's. Is she in danger? Or might she be harboring dangerous secrets?

Todd Kavanaugh — An armed robbery suspect caught with the same type of firearm used by the serial killer. Is he the unsub they're looking for?

Joaquin Kalember — A known sex offender with a history of violence. But is he also a serial killer?

Bends Lake Predator — A callous serial killer who shoots his victims to death and believes he is clever enough to get away with it, while setting his sights on Stella.

Prologue

Peggy Elizondo had only recently moved to the picturesque town of Bends Lake, Kansas—some four hours' drive from Kansas City in the state—where she'd landed a teaching job at Bends Lake Middle School. Fresh from receiving her secondary teacher certification from the University of North Texas, a month shy of turning twenty-two, she welcomed the opportunity to prove her worth in the classroom and beyond. As a proud member of the Kickapoo Traditional Tribe of Texas, she fully intended to connect with the Kickapoo Tribe in Kansas to stay close to her roots and, indeed, extend them. But for now, she was just happy to do her thing, which included fixing up her brand-new one-bedroom apartment on Fennkel Road and taking full advantage of the summer activities afforded her in the community.

Peggy's long and curly brunette ponytail swung from side to side while she jogged spiritedly through the eastern cottonwood trees surrounding the winding runner's trail in Blakely Park, which bordered the popular and recreational Lake Bends and seemed to have no end in sight. That worked for her, as she loved pushing herself to the limit as part of her fitness routine. Unfortunately, the same sentiment wasn't true when it came to her love life.

Once a cheater, always a cheater. Or at least she chose to abide by this old adage in breaking up with her no-good boyfriend, Chip McBride, last month after catching him in bed with another woman. Though he called it a big mistake and said he deeply regretted it and swore it wouldn't happen again, their trust had been irreparably broken. She wasn't about to allow him to hurt her again.

If she was lucky, someone else was waiting around the proverbial corner to come into her life, putting even more distance between her and Chip.

A girl can still dream, can't she? Peggy thought imaginatively, as she sucked in a deep breath and cast her big brown eyes at the abundant nature all around her. *I could really get used to this*, she told herself. She wondered if the nightlife in Bends Lake was as generous. Maybe she would put it to the test this weekend and see if she could make a connection with someone.

Only in that moment did Peggy break out of her reverie at the sound of branches snapping in the near distance, as if whispering to her. Perhaps another runner coming or going? Or maybe some, hopefully friendly, wildlife making its or their way home?

She suddenly stopped in her tracks, as if hitting a wall, as Peggy saw a tall and muscular white male seem to come out of nowhere—he'd actually stepped out from between trees up ahead—effectively and deliberately blocking her way down the path. On a quick perusal, she supposed she would consider him handsome, if not exactly her type. He was dark-haired, blue-eyed and wearing dark clothing and gloves, along with dirty white running shoes. She guessed him to be in his mid to late thirties. Only now did she notice that he was holding a firearm.

And pointing it directly at her.

How had she missed this?

The obvious answer was that he must have slipped it out of the pocket of his windbreaker jacket as she was sizing him up.

So...what? He wanted to rape or rob her in broad daylight? Take her cell phone? Steal her car? *Good luck with that*, Peggy told herself, knowing that she had jogged to the park directly from her apartment. So her Toyota Corolla was safe.

But what about herself?

She considered that he may want to actually kill her, for one reason or another.

Or any combination of the possibilities laid out in her head could be in play.

Whichever way she sliced it, Peggy recognized that her predicament didn't look good. And that was putting it quite mildly. She was in deep trouble. Fighting back the fear that gripped her like an angry parent, she tried to take control of her emotions and keep a cool head under the obvious fire that stood curiously before her without uttering a word as yet.

Maybe if she spoke to him first—tried to reason with him as a newbie in town who just wanted a chance to make a decent life for herself in Bends Lake—he would turn his attention elsewhere and leave her alone. Was that truly asking too much?

When she managed to get something to come out of her trembling lips, Peggy couldn't prevent herself from stammering, as she said, "P-please d-don't hurt me—"

The man snickered at her with what appeared to be amusement and responded sarcastically, "I won't." He waited a beat and added in a harsher inflection, "At least not in the way you may be most dreading—short of death…"

Peggy considered his words. He seemed to be reading her mind as it related to the fear of being sexually assaulted. Or beaten up. She hated the thought of being violated, humiliated or left in agony.

But if those were off the table, it left only one thing that played on perhaps her worst fears, like the fear in childhood of being accosted by a monster with very bad intentions hiding under the bed.

"Unfortunately, you *are* about to die," the man snorted wickedly in confirming his deadly intentions, as he kept the barrel of the handgun aimed squarely at her chest. "And I'm afraid there's really nothing you can do about it—any more than those who came before you… Except maybe say a prayer or whatever you think may give you some comfort in your last moments of life and whatever comes after—"

Peggy winced. So, there were other victims caught in the same deadly trap? With nowhere to turn to escape the inevitable. Fueled by that terrible realization and refusing to succumb to it, she decided that her only chance—slim as it was—of coming out of this alive was to make a run for it. Straight toward him, hopefully catching the man off guard just enough to throw him off—while screaming at the top of her lungs for someone, anyone, to hear—and using her speed to try and escape the assailant through the trees.

Only she hadn't counted on him being one step ahead of her. Maybe two. Or three, as it turned out.

Like a trained assassin, he opened fire, hitting her once in the chest. Then twice.

Strangely, she barely heard any sounds coming from the gun. He must have used some type of silencer. Either that, or she had somehow lost her hearing in the process of being shot.

As she went down like a ton of bricks—or the target of a vicious right hook by a heavyweight prizefighter—Peggy lay sprawled on the solid ground, clutching her chest as if this would somehow alleviate the tremendous damage done to her insides. Or the incredible pain that tore through her as if she'd been struck by a Mack truck.

When her attacker stood above her, clearly gloating over what he had done, all she could manage to utter out of her contorted mouth, with blood spurting out, was, "Wh-why...d-did you d-do this...sh-shoot me...?" Not that she expected an answer. Or would accept anything that legitimized murdering her in cold blood and depriving her of the new life she had made for herself in Bends Lake.

But he did respond, after a boastful chuckle. "Because, as the Bends Lake Predator, this is what I do—for reasons you couldn't begin to understand." He furrowed his brow thoughtfully then laughed again. "Honestly, I just can't help myself..."

The Bends Lake Predator? What did he mean? Peggy tried to decipher the words, as if they were spoken in a foreign language, even as she lay dying in a pool of her own blood. A dogged perpetrator who hunted human beings as prey for whatever sick fantasies he had? Or was there some other deep meaning to the description?

Turning back to herself, Peggy couldn't help but think about her lost future and what might have been. Had it not been for her misfortune of becoming the target of a killer.

Her attacker continued, "If it hadn't been you, trust me, it would have been someone else. Actually, it has been. One after another over time…" He chuckled, even more wickedly than before, at his own warped smugness. "So sad. Too bad."

As it began to dawn on Peggy just what he meant, and how she must have somehow found herself in the crosshairs of a serial killer, he aimed the gun at her once more and fired another shot, before everything went completely black.

THE BENDS LAKE PREDATOR took a moment to gape at the pretty dead woman, imagining what her very last thought had been before her life was snuffed out for good. Maybe she was hoping for some sort of miracle to happen—manmade or otherwise—whereby she was able to cheat death and get on with her existence.

Surely that was what the others who came before her were praying for as well.

Like them, her last-ditch Hail Mary for a successful escape fell short. No one would come to stop him just in the nick of time. He made sure of that.

He did what had to be done.

And would do so again at a time and place of his choosing. Always one step ahead of the game, he relished outmaneuvering those who tried in vain to stop him.

Maintaining control and confidence was in his DNA, no matter the obstacles that always threatened to stand in his way.

He tucked the Springfield Armory 1911 Ronin Operator 9 mm pistol with a suppressor away in his waistband, hidden inside his jacket, and left the corpse for others to come upon, to their horror. And his expectation.

Backtracking through the woods, making sure he was neither seen nor heard, he waited till he was a safe distance from the scene of the crime and prying eyes before stepping out into the open. Running a hand through his thick hair innocently, he effortlessly blended in with other park goers, offering a deceptive friendly grin here and there and getting one in return.

When he reached his vehicle, the Bends Lake Predator climbed inside calmly, started the engine and drove off scot-free. while, admittedly, much more treacherous than anyone could ever suspect.

Chapter One

Looks like the Bends Lake Predator is at it once again. Declan Delgado replayed the ominous words mentally from Ursula Liebert, his fellow Kansas Bureau of Investigation special agent within the KBI Field Investigations Division. She had phoned him from Blakely Park, where the body of a female runner had been discovered less than an hour ago on this afternoon in mid-August. According to Ursula, she had been shot to death at close range, reminiscent of the modus operandi of who they believed was an adult white male serial killer prowling Bends Lake like a ruthless predator on a mission. The unsub had been given the chilling moniker *Bends Lake Predator* by the press. Declan found it more than a little frustrating that the perpetrator was somehow, some way, able to adeptly evade detection, leaving no workable clues or solid forensic or physical evidence to identify him. The killer targeted women and men before cunningly sliding back into anonymity and his normal life till it was time to strike again.

If the current homicide victim panned out as one of his, that would mean that the Bends Lake Predator had murdered six people in the last six months. This didn't sit well with Declan as he drove down Belle Lane toward the park in his duty vehicle, a mineral-gray metallic Chevrolet Malibu. The KBI had taken the lead in the investigation, as part of a Bends Lake Predator Task Force operation that included detectives and crime scene investigators from the Bends Lake Police Department and Danver County Sheriff's Office. Though no one was bumping heads, per se, the serial killer was still very much at large, much to their chagrin, and apparently hiding in plain view while eyeing new potential targets to take out.

I hate that he's clearly got the upper hand right now, so long as the unsub keeps from slipping up, Declan mused, before he cursed back the thought. But that could only last for so long. His penchant for wanting to see each and every investigation successful in terms of slapping handcuffs on the perp or eliminating them as a threat if there was no surrender had been there ever since he joined the KBI nine years ago. Before that, he had worked for the Kansas City, Kansas, Police Department as a homicide detective after receiving his bachelor's degree from the School of Criminal Justice at Wichita State University.

After losing his parents at an early age in the state's capital city of Topeka and being bounced between relatives while trying to keep his head above water when he could very easily have fallen in with the wrong crowd, Declan managed to buck the trend of some he'd grown up with. He had fought hard to stay on the right side of the tracks, determined to do something good with his life and make a difference in the lives of others.

Declan's thoughts turned to currently being an unexpected widower at the relatively young age of thirty-six. How could anyone be prepared to deal with losing one's wife the way he did three years ago, when Elise's Dodge Hornet had been hit head on by a speeding, out-of-control drunk driver? They had barely been married for four years, after a whirlwind romance saw them go down the aisle. But fate had found a way to stomp all over his life, while cruelly taking away hers.

To make matters worse for Declan, in ways he hated to admit—but couldn't run away from even if he wanted to—was that he had been involved with Elise's older sister, Stella Bailey, prior to meeting and hitting it off with Elise, an attractive divorcée. He had ended things with Stella before he started dating Elise—or even knew they were siblings for that matter—believing that there was no real future with her gorgeous but ambitious and career-minded sister. But he didn't exactly ingratiate himself with Stella when Declan asked Elise to marry him. While she seemed to want her younger sister to be happy in all ways possible, that same sentiment didn't necessarily apply to him, which Stella made plainly obvious by giving him the cold shoulder from that point on.

Elise's untimely and tragic death had only strained things between them that much more, as though Stella somehow blamed him for what happened to her sister. Or at least it appeared that way to Declan, as she cut him out of her life altogether like a surgeon would a deadly cancer in the body—as if he'd never been a part of it in the first place—giving him essentially no say in the matter. Out of respect for her, albeit it against his own wishes, he abided by Stella's apparent desire not to have anything to do with him anymore.

I can only wonder what might have been had things

worked out between me and Stella before I ever got into a relationship with her sister, Declan told himself as he drove into the park. Maybe he should have been more patient with Stella. Given them a fighting chance, even if they were on different career paths, though both in law enforcement. Or would he have only prolonged the inevitable, which wouldn't have been good for either of them?

He even wondered if—in some strange quirk of nature—Elise might still be alive today had he not married her and, by virtue, inadvertently set the fatal chain of events in motion. After all, Elise had been on her way to their house after a quick trip to the supermarket to pick up some things for dinner. But had she been single and uninvolved with him, she might have taken a different route or not even have lived in Bends Lake at all that fateful day.

Don't even go there, Declan admonished himself as reality set in. No matter how he tried to play it, no amount of guilt was justifiable in trying to rewrite history with what-ifs.

He parked in the lot, cut off the ignition and checked the leather holster on his side for the loaded SIG Sauer P226 9 mm semiautomatic pistol before getting out of the car. At six foot two and a half, he was probably in the best shape of his life thanks to regular workouts at the gym, on an outside basketball court and elsewhere. After making his way inside the park, Declan flashed his identification to get beyond the yellow crime scene barricade tape and officers on hand, where he then conferred with the KBI Crime Scene Response Team, which was collecting and preserving evidence, photographing the scene and performing more of their duties.

Declan spotted Ursula Liebert, who saw him at the same time, and they approached each other. Ursula was tall and slender, with light blond hair in a blunt cut that fell just below her shoulders. The thirty-two-year-old special agent and her pregnant British wife, Melody, were expecting their first child soon. It was something he envied, given that his own dream of having children had been dealt a serious blow. He'd lost Elise before they even had a chance to get to that point in their marriage. No one he'd dated since then—and there hadn't been that many—gave him any reason to believe that equation would change anytime soon. And prior to his relationship with Elise, things had never even come close to progressing into that type of discussion when Declan was seeing Stella, before they went their separate ways.

"Hey," Ursula said evenly, snapping him out of his reverie as she stood before him.

"Hey." Declan met her clear blue eyes. "What's the latest?" he asked, wanting details over and beyond what had already been relayed to him about the apparent homicide.

"Victim's a Hispanic or Native American female in her early twenties, shot three times at close range, fatally… We're still trying to identify her." Ursula paused. "Dressed in jogging clothes. I'm guessing she was doing just that before she was ambushed by someone—"

Declan pinched his nose while musing. "Who discovered the body?"

"Another jogger… Yasmine Yoshiko. Apparently, she was caught up in her own thoughts when spotting the victim, nearly tripping over her body lying on the trail. She called 911 right away."

"Did she happen to run into anyone else along the way—or after the fact?" Declan had to ask.

"According to Ms. Yoshiko, she had just begun her run and hadn't seen anyone coming or going on the trail up to that point."

"Lucky her." Declan knew that if she had come face to face with the killer, particularly if the unsub was the serial predator they suspected him to be and she could identify him, Yasmine Yoshiko would also most likely be dead right now. "We'll see what surveillance cameras in the park or local area can give us."

"Hopefully something," Ursula said with a sigh. "Along with whatever the CSRT discovers beyond the shell casings found near the victim."

Thoughtful, Declan scratched his pate below short dark hair. "So, where's the body?"

Ursula wrinkled her nose. "Right through those trees—" she pointed at the rows of eastern cottonwoods "—just as the trail curves. The medical examiner has arrived and is with the deceased now."

"Let's have a look." Declan followed her to the crime scene, where he regarded the victim lying awkwardly on her back as she was being tended to on the dirt trail. She was slender and wearing an orange running tank, brown athletic shorts and white-and-orange sneakers. Her brunette ponytail was lying to the side, soaked in her own blood. There was a bullet wound in her forehead and two wounds in her chest.

The Danver County medical examiner and coroner was Dr. Aaron Wilson. African American, he was in his midforties and of medium build, with gray-black hair in a short Afro. Crouching, he lifted sable eyes behind horn-rimmed glasses to Declan and acknowledged him naturally. "Agent Delgado."

"Doc Wilson." Declan nodded at him, wishing circumstances hadn't called for them to become better acquainted of late, then cut to the chase. "Where do things stand in your assessment of the situation?"

Flexing his large hands covered with nitrile gloves, the medical examiner took a breath and responded, "Well, pending the official autopsy report, I can tell you that the decedent was shot three times at close range, with the shot to the head likely the one that killed her. Though two shots to the chest would ultimately have had the same effect..." He glanced at the victim. "No early indications of defensive wounds, suggesting she didn't even have a chance to put up a decent fight before dying where she lay."

"What's your preliminary estimate on the time of death?" Declan asked, presuming it had to be close to the time she was discovered by the other runner. Still, he wanted to have an official general timeline on the victim's whereabouts prior to her demise to consider how this could have been used against her.

Without seeming to give it much thought, Wilson answered matter-of-factly, "I'd say the decedent died instantly once the fatal shot occurred, likely within the last couple of hours..."

Which gave her killer just enough leeway to flee the scene of the crime and find a safe haven away from the murder, Declan told himself as he watched the medical examiner and coroner get to his feet and order his team to lift the victim's body onto a stretcher to take her away.

THE FOLLOWING MORNING, Declan sat on a leather swivel chair in his office at the KBI office on Washington Street in Great Bend, Kansas. Great Bend was the county seat of Barton County and around twenty miles or so from the crime scene in Bends Lake. He had just gotten word from the Firearm and Toolmark Section of the forensic science laboratory in the building, after the ballistics evidence had been transferred there from the Evidence Control Center. It confirmed what he had expected. The bullets that killed the as yet unidentified woman in Blakely Park matched the cartridge cases left at the scene and were linked to the same Springfield Armory 1911 Ronin Operator 9 mm handgun and bullets used in five other murders committed by the Bends Lake Predator. In spite of the correlation and cross referencing of the ballistic evidence when loaded into the Bureau of Alcohol, Tobacco, Firearms and Explosives National Integrated Ballistic Information Network, the actual murder weapon had yet to be recovered for analysis.

It is obviously still in the possession of the unsub, Declan thought perceptively. Waiting to be used again on one or more unsuspecting victims while the nameless killer remained on the loose. And was as dangerous as ever.

This told Declan that—their capabilities in law enforcement within the Bends Lake Predator Task Force notwithstanding—they could use some help from the feds in solving the serial killer case. Or more specifically, the type of assistance that a well-respected profiler might be able to give them in getting a better grip on the perp and his way of thinking.

Stella Bailey came to mind. He knew she was certainly at the top of her game when it came to criminal behavioral analysis, having kept track of his sister-in-law's efforts in this area from a safe—if not uncomfortable—distance since she relocated to Detroit, Michigan.

Would she be up to returning to Bends Lake to work with him and the team, in spite of their frosty and all but nonexistent relationship since—and even before—Elise's death? At this point, even getting Stella to consult remotely would be welcome, given her expertise in criminal profiling.

Or was either option too much to ask? Or for that matter, did he even have the right to expect anything, considering the tragedy that made the divide between them greater and, he sensed, damned near impossible to repair?

Only one way to find out, Declan told himself determinedly. He felt desperation—but just as much a desire to try and make things right between them on at least some level after three years—as he got on the phone with the FBI's field office in Detroit.

STELLA BAILEY SAT in an ergonomic chair at the L-shaped desk in her office on the twenty-sixth floor of the Federal Bureau of Investigation's Detroit field office on Michigan Avenue. The FBI behavioral analyst's sharp brown eyes were gazing at the notes on her laptop. Or more specifically, the profile she had developed on the Montana mass shooter who had used an AR-15 semiautomatic rifle to kill ten people at a crowded shopping center last month in Cascade County before escaping the carnage. This led to the unsub being positively identified as Leonard Fetterman, a vengeful estranged husband. His wife, Stefi, along with the man she was dating, were among the victims. Fetterman was ultimately taken into custody without incident, seemingly feeling that the deadly act more than justified the means for him and whatever came next.

Stella sighed. She never failed to be amazed at the audacity of some perps in believing they had a right to take the lives of others. And worse, that they were able to outsmart everyone else in the process. Till their misdeeds and overconfidence caught up with them in the end. She was more than happy to play a role—big or small—in taking such despicable offenders down as a criminal profiler, having worked on cases across the United States and even on loan abroad on occasion, when called upon. Ever since she graduated from the University of Kansas in Lawrence with a master of arts in psychology nearly a decade ago, Stella knew it was her calling to use this educational pursuit to dig into violent criminal behavior and the deviant minds of the perpetrators. Which was why she'd joined the FBI as a special agent, after successfully completing the grueling Special Agent Selection System process. Her position was boosted as she made her way to the Bureau's Behavioral Analysis Unit, with a focus on criminal investigative analysis and identifying what made offenders tick—as both a prelude to their downfall and after the fact, in order to use their characteristics to help identify and capture other dangerous criminals. She had used her knowledge to write two successful books on criminal profiling and was currently under contract to write a third book.

Beyond that, Stella felt that it had always been in her DNA to be there for those she cared about on a more personal level. Starting with her sister, Elise. Both were biracial, with a beautiful English American mother and handsome white father. Elise, two years younger than Stella, had sadly passed away before her time three years ago, which somehow seemed like forever and only yesterday at the same time.

After Elise's death, Stella's heartbroken parents, Ngozi and Lester Bailey, had moved from their hometown of Bends Lake, Kansas, to Detroit, Michigan, to escape the memories and have a fresh start—both taking jobs as professors at Wayne State University. Though she had moved around for her career, Stella would eventually follow suit when taking a job at the Bureau's Detroit field office in hopes of trying to fill the void in her parents' lives in the absence of one of their precious daughters.

But what about the giant void in her own life? At thirty-three years of age, she had been left to fend for herself, without her sister—or a meaningful romance, with no one in the picture to cozy up to at night at the moment. Not that she hadn't gone out on the occasional date that went nowhere. Or didn't want someone special in her life. After having that once years ago, only to lose him when she least expected it, she had come to believe that maybe it just wasn't in the cards for her to find true and enduring love. So instead, work had pretty much become her focal point these days.

At least that's something I can always count on, for better or worse, Stella told herself, though she was also committed to doing her best to be there for her mother and father. She broke out of her reverie as her boss, Valerie Izbicki, entered the office. The petite forty-six-year-old assistant special agent in charge had been in the post for the past two years, and Stella was certain it was only a matter of time before she was promoted to the position of special agent in charge in one field office or another.

"Hey," Stella said tentatively, eyeing her while running a hand through her long, layered black hair.

"Hey." Valerie smiled thinly, her short blond shag a good fit for an oval face and green eyes. She had on round glasses and touched them. "So, I've got a new assignment for you..."

"Okay." Though barely past her last assignment and the one before that, Stella wasn't about to complain, having gotten used to going wherever she was needed as part of the job. "Where to this time?" She considered that she may be able to lend her expertise remotely in making good use of today's advanced video conferencing capabilities.

"Actually, it's Bends Lake." Valerie waited a beat as if to gauge her reaction. "Your hometown, right?"

"Yes." Stella smoothed a thin brow, ill at ease as the painful memories came to the surface.

"The request came from the Kansas Bureau of Investigation," the assistant special agent in charge pointed out.

"The KBI?" Stella asked.

"They're investigating a serial killer on the loose there. You may have heard about it through the grapevine?"

"Actually, I hadn't," Stella confessed. Apart from deliberately avoiding keeping tabs on the happenings in the town she grew up in, she had been preoccupied with other cases, including a serial killer of children she'd profiled recently in Michigan's Upper Peninsula. Still, she cringed at the thought of a serial killer at large in

Bends Lake, even while hesitant to return there for her own reasons.

As if sensing her reluctance, Valerie said, "Normally, we would assign an analyst based at or near the FBI Kansas City field office, but you were specifically requested by the KBI special agent working the case, Declan Delgado, so I figured you'd want this one. If not, tell me now, no questions asked…"

Stella's first instincts had been to take the opening she was being given and pass on the assignment with a firm no. Or, at the very least, request that she offer her analysis from afar, knowing her physical presence would not be truly needed if the digital files were sent to her.

But then that would mean she was acting on emotions rather than in her professional capacity. Was that how she wanted to play this? She imagined that Valerie was purposely putting her to the test, to see her limits. And probably the same was true with the KBI agent requesting her presence.

"Declan's my brother-in-law," Stella informed her boss matter-of-factly, assuming that he hadn't volunteered this information when requesting her services.

"Seriously?" Valerie fluttered her lashes, as if totally in the dark about it.

Stella nodded. "He was married to my sister, Elise, who died in a car accident three years ago."

"Sorry to hear that." Valerie's brow creased. "I can only imagine how difficult it must have been for both of you."

I doubt you could imagine just how difficult it truly was on multiple levels, Stella told herself. Still, she wished she had mentioned it before now, but there never seemed to be a good reason to do so. Now that the cat was out of the bag, she needed to deal with it.

"I'll return to Bends Lake and do what I can to help with the investigation," Stella told her without giving it much more thought. That would come later.

Valerie nodded without probing further and said, "The KC field office in Kansas City, Missouri, will be sending over a couple of FBI special agents to join the task force as well, as part of the Bureau's cooperation on the case."

"Okay." Stella wondered if she might know the assigned agents, having been based at that field office at one point.

"You leave this afternoon."

All Stella could think to say in response was "Then I guess I better go pack a few things."

"Good luck," Valerie said, as if she would need it, and left the office.

Stella glanced at a framed photograph on her desk and picked it up. It was of her and Elise, who was beautiful, with long blond hair in a razored shag style and big hazel eyes. The pic was taken when they were in their early twenties and the future seemed endless.

Until it wasn't.

She grabbed her nylon hobo bag and headed home.

Chapter Two

Stella drove her blue Ford Edge SUV back to the townhouse she lived in on Orleans Street. It was filled with contemporary furnishings, had hickory hardwood flooring and plenty of windows with natural sunlight streaming through the venetian blinds.

After packing her bags with probably more than she needed for what Stella expected to be a relatively short trip, she called her parents and informed them that she would be headed to Bends Lake for a few days on business.

As expected, they were surprised but fully supportive of her returning home to come face to face with Declan again—whom they had kept in touch with as part of seeking to keep the memory of Elise alive. For her part, Stella viewed the personal aspect of the visit with an awareness that there were uncomfortable questions that needed to be answered, one way or another.

She got on a Delta flight and was seated by the window, where Stella stared out at the clouds, meditative, and for good reason. Or bad, depending on how she looked at it.

Seven years ago, she had dated Declan Delgado for a few months, hitting it off right away with the handsome

Hispanic KBI special agent and finding him seemingly on the same wavelength in most instances. It ended all too soon in Stella's mind. Unbeknownst to her, he had turned his attention to Elise, who fell hard for Declan and vice versa, with him eventually asking her to marry him.

Elise, who had been in a brief marriage to her college sweetheart, Roland Goldoni, said yes, dashing any hopes Stella had still harbored for resuming a relationship with Declan. This reality prompted her to transfer to a different field office for work, believing that distance between her and the newlyweds was best all the way around, while wanting Elise to get everything she deserved in a husband the second time around.

They had only been married for four years when tragedy struck like an earthquake, leaving Declan a widower and Stella without her beloved only sibling. She distanced herself from the man Elise gave her heart to, feeling it was too painful to maintain anything resembling close contact. She hadn't been back to Bends Lake since Elise's funeral three years ago, and Stella wasn't quite sure what to expect. Or not to, for that matter. *I don't want to overthink this*, she thought, thin fingers running through her hair while barely realizing it. Or presume that Declan handpicked her to profile the unsub for all the wrong reasons.

I have a job to do, and that's what this is all about, Stella told herself. All that was important at the moment was to see if she could provide the task force with enough insight into a serial killer and hope it was enough to help bring him to justice. Surely Declan did not have ulterior motives in wanting to see her again?

After arriving at Great Bend Municipal Airport, Stella

rented a silver Mitsubishi Outlander and drove to the nearby town of Bends Lake, which she had once called home. She took in the familiar scenery—and unfamiliar in some areas—including mature maple tree-lined streets; Cape Cod, boutique, manufactured and historic homes; new construction and rich farmland.

In turning right on Burtiford Avenue, Stella knew that had she turned left, she would have come upon Bends Lake Hospital, where Elise had worked as an occupational therapist. Passing by Bends Lake High School, which Stella once attended, along with Elise, a touch of sadness swept over her at the thought that Elise would never get to attend her twenty- or twenty-five-year reunion.

A couple of minutes later, Stella checked into the Kotton Hotel on Lake Way. She took the elevator up to her fifth-floor suite. After going inside, she scanned the place and saw that it had a separate nice-size living area with plush beige carpeting and a window wall behind cordless blinds, along with contemporary furniture. The amenities included a flat-screen television, microwave, mini fridge and granite wet bar.

Stella took a walk through the spacious corner bedroom with a queen bed and another television and an en suite bathroom before stepping out on the balcony that overlooked Lake Bends and gazing at the forty-five-acre lake that had a fishing dock, boating, swimming and an adjoining nature trail. She recalled spending time on and in the water with Elise and their friends.

No sooner had she gone back inside and started to unpack her belongings—including the Glock 19 Gen5 9x19 mm compact duty pistol, which she put away in the bottom drawer of the walnut dresser—when there was a knock on the door. Deciding she was presentable enough while still wearing her casual flight attire and flats, Stella walked to it, thinking someone from the hotel might be checking to see if she needed anything.

Only when she opened the door, Stella laid her eyes on the tall and firmly built person who was, she hated to admit, still as handsome as ever. Honestly, she had once wondered if she would ever see him again.

Declan Delgado.

"Declan..." Her voice shook as she tried to get his name out while gawking at his square-jawed face and deep brown eyes with enticing gray flecks. His coarse black hair was in a high and tight style. He was dressed in a navy blazer over a light blue button-down shirt, dark pants and black loafers.

"Hi, Stella." His own voice was smooth, calm and collected. "It's been a minute."

"Actually, more like three years," she replied sarcastically, though suspecting he knew as much, considering the circumstances. How did he know where she was staying?

"Yeah, time flies." He brushed his Roman nose thoughtfully, then read her mind as he said, "I was told where to find you by my contact at the Bureau—and when you would arrive."

It took Stella a moment to regain her equilibrium. "I see."

He grinned askance. "Thanks for coming."

"I wasn't given much of a choice," she told him tartly, even if this wasn't exactly true. "My boss has a bad habit of cooperating when our assistance is requested in investigations."

"Guess some habits, good and bad, are hard to break," he quipped, museful. "Appreciate it, nonetheless."

Don't make a big deal out of coming home and seeing him again, Stella scolded herself. She needed to put professionalism above all else. Softening her tone, she said, "I'll do whatever I can to help with the case."

"I was counting on that." Declan eyed her with a straight look. "With your expertise in criminal profiling, I'm sure you'll be able to shed some light on the unsub we're after and just what we're dealing with here." He waited a beat before asking, "Mind if I come in?"

For whatever reason—actually, she could think of one or two but kept them to herself—Stella didn't think that was such a good idea and responded accordingly. "There's a coffee shop downstairs. Why don't I meet you there instead? Just give me a few minutes to freshen up."

"Not a problem." His jaw tightened. "See you then."

Stella watched him walk away for a moment, before closing the door and leaning her back against it broodingly. She couldn't fault Elise for wanting to be with Declan as his wife, as Stella knew full well the many admirable qualities he possessed as a man. Any more than she could fault him for choosing her sister to be his bride. Elise was beautiful, smart and a good catch for any pursuer—having moved back to Bends Lake upon getting her master of occupational therapy degree from the University of Kansas. She would also have been a wonderful mother, had fate not intervened.

Stella could only imagine what else might have been in store for her sister, had Elise been able to live a full life. *I'm sure that Declan's also wondering the same thing,* she told herself. Even if he had moved on with his life—and romantic interests, undoubtedly. She sucked in a deep breath and headed toward the bedroom.

After washing her face, putting her hair up and quickly changing her clothing, Stella grabbed her small leather handbag and left the room while feeling a little nervous at the prospect of getting together with Declan again.

DECLAN WAS ADMITTEDLY on pins and needles as he sat at a table in Kendre's Coffee Café, sipping on brewed coffee, while awaiting Stella. Truthfully, he hadn't even been sure she would come back to Bends Lake, if it meant they would have to have a conversation on everything from breaking up to marrying her sister and Elise's death. He half—maybe more than that—expected Stella to find a way out of the assignment.

Yet here she was, meaning that they both would need to come to terms with some things, apart from whatever Stella could bring to the Bends Lake Predator investigation.

Declan watched as she walked toward the table, looking every bit as gorgeous as the day he first laid eyes on her. A diamond-shaped face with a beautiful complexion was taut, with attractive small brown eyes, a button nose and full lips proportionately situated. Long raven hair was in a high ponytail with curly layered strands bordering her face. She was now wearing a white satin top, brown knit trousers and low-heeled black pumps.

"Hey," Declan said, offering her a soft smile.

Stella responded evenly, "Hey."

"I took the liberty of ordering you a latte," he told her

as she sat on a wooden chair. "I assume that's what you still like in coffee?"

"Yes, it is," she confirmed. "Thank you." She lifted the mug and took a sip.

"No problem." Declan tasted his own coffee. *At least it's nice to know that some things never change*, he thought. "So, how have you been?"

Stella sipped more coffee thoughtfully. "Busy," she responded simply. "My life has been anything but boring."

He could take that in more ways than one but decided not to ask just yet about her love life, feeling it was probably inappropriate. Still, imagining her with another man was uncomfortable, even if he had absolutely no right to resent Stella moving on with her life in whatever way she saw fit.

Declan brushed that thought aside. "Yeah, I suppose that working as a special agent for the Bureau, and especially profiling different villains as part of the process, can be a demanding job."

"It can be," she conceded, then turned the tables on him. "How are things with you these days?"

"Also busy, chasing the bad guys and trying my damnedest to not let them slip through the cracks," he responded, while thinking, *Wish I could say I'd found someone new to share my life with, but that isn't the case*. Not that this was something he figured she had any interest in at this stage.

Stella regarded him. "You mean like the so-called Bends Lake Predator?" She paused, adding, "I did a cursory glance at your investigation through news accounts while on the plane."

"Yeah, that would certainly be at the top of my current

caseload," Declan told her. "So far, the unsub's managed to stay on the deadly offensive while adroitly avoiding capture. I'm hoping that the more we can get into his psyche, the better the chance of identifying and nailing him before he kills again—"

"I understand." She flipped one of the cute curls from her brow. "I'm ready to learn more about the unsub and where the investigation is at this point."

"Good to know," he said, putting the mug to his lips. "As it is, we're about to give an update on the case and look forward to your assessment of the serial killer."

"You'll have it," she promised, "with the obvious caveat that characterizing an offender can only go so far in getting to the root of the criminal behavior. Not to mention, any unsub is capable of changing his or her patterns of conduct at any time."

"Understood." Declan liked being able to speak with her again, even if on a professional level. If he had any say in it, they would go beyond that while the opportunity presented itself. He leaned forward. "Look, I know the Bureau is footing the bill for the hotel—but, just so you know, you're more than welcome to stay at the house while you're here. There's plenty of room…" Was he really trying to put pressure on her to let bygones be bygones?

"Thanks for the offer." Stella looked at him for a moment. "But I think it's probably best all the way around that I stay put during the short time I'm in town. So if it's all right with you, I'll pass."

"Of course." Declan hid his unrealistic disappointment. "Whatever works for you." He wouldn't push it.

"Well, if you don't mind riding with me, I'll drive you to and from the police department."

She flashed a tiny smile. "I'm fine with that."

"Okay." He would take every small victory that came his way in the slow thaw of the wall of ice between them, if he was reading this correctly.

IN A CONFERENCE room at the Bends Lake Police Department on Sorenten Street, Declan stood in the front, eager to get started. He glanced at the three individuals standing beside him and said affably, "I'd like to welcome to the Bends Lake Predator Task Force FBI special agents Stella Bailey, Keene Haverstock and Arielle Mendoza. Agents Haverstock and Mendoza are from the Bureau's Kansas City field office, and Agent Bailey is a well-known FBI behavioral analyst out of Detroit, who just happens to be my sister-in-law." He swept over that quickly, wanting to be transparent while also dismissing it as irrelevant to her involvement in the case. "Their participation in the investigation will hopefully bring us closer to wrapping up the case and holding the unsub fully accountable for everything he's done in Bends Lake—"

He shook hands with the three, starting with Keene Haverstock—who was in his midforties, tall and muscular, and had a gray high-fade haircut—followed by Arielle Mendoza—an attractive and curvy Latina in her early thirties with brunette hair in a pixie wedge. Declan finished with Stella. He wrapped his large hand around her small hand with thin fingers and felt a tingle of memory course through him as they locked eyes. Had she felt it too?

If so, it must have stung, as Stella released their hands almost as quickly as they grasped one another. Declan accepted her resistance to—or defense mechanism against—anything that suggested more of a personal relationship between them than strictly coworkers. He understood the delicate lines that neither of them wanted to cross given their prior connection.

As the special agents stepped away and found somewhere to sit, Declan motioned for KBI special agent Ursula Liebert to join him in getting to the main crux of the meeting. After grabbing the stylus pen from the rectangular conference table, Declan gazed at a large touch screen display and placed on it a collage of six photographs of individuals taken while they were still alive and well.

He glanced at Stella and then, largely to give her everything he could to work with, said, "In the past six months, these six persons have been shot to death in Bends Lake by an unknown assailant. Three men. Three women. It still remains to be seen if this was calculated. Or happenstance."

Declan clicked on one picture, which then occupied the screen all by itself. It was of an attractive white female with curly red hair in a collarbone blunt cut and blue eyes.

"Erica Reilly, a thirty-nine-year-old caterer, was gunned down outside her home on Vale Lane, as the first victim linked to the unsub we're calling the Bends Lake Predator—on account of his brazen display of violence and ability to slither away like the poisonous snake that he is and make himself scarce from detection and apprehension, while leaving no positively identifying DNA or fingerprints at the crime scene."

He selected the next image of an Asian male with a black faux hawk hairstyle and brown eyes, and said, "Victim number two was Henry Minnillo, a twenty-five-year-old software engineer, shot and killed after visiting a friend at the Leighwood apartment complex on Roiten Road." Declan went to another picture—this one an African American female who had platinum hair in a fluffy Afro and black eyes. "The next victim was thirty-six-year-old Gwendolyn Gunderson, a cabaret singer who was shot to death shortly after a performance at a jazz club on Twenty-third Street."

Declan let that sink in for a moment before switching to the fourth person to become a victim of gunfire. He glanced at the gray-haired white male with green eyes and said, "Billy Rottenberg, forty, a construction supervisor, was shot and killed outside a building his company was constructing on Jenkins Lane." Declan immediately moved on to the next image of a young Hispanic male with long and stringy brown hair and dark eyes. "The fifth victim was nineteen-year-old college student Erique Ruiz, who was shot when he was walking along Warline Road, blocks away from Bends Lake University."

Switching to the most recent victim, who had attractive brown eyes and long brunette hair, he said, "Yesterday morning, Peggy Elizondo, a twenty-one-year-old Native American middle school teacher, was gunned down while jogging in Blakely Park." Declan sighed, expressing his discontent. "All six victims were shot at point-blank range three times—the last shot of which was a kill shot to the head. Needless to say, the unsub shows no signs of slowing down. Not till we force the issue, one way or the other—"

With that, Declan stepped aside, turning the stylus over to Ursula, who flashed him an even look and quickly brought up on the monitor a firearm. "All six of the murder victims were shot to death with a Springfield Armory 1911 Ronin Operator 9 mm pistol—much like the one you see on the screen," she said smoothly. "The bullets were fired from a gun barrel with six lands and grooves that had a right-hand twist. Based upon the lack of sound as reported by witnesses and others nearby, we believe that the gun was likely equipped with a sound suppressor." She put one on the screen as an example. "Though the actual murder weapon is not yet in our possession, we're confident that this is only a matter of time. Just as it is before we identify the culprit and put an end to his reign of terror in Bends Lake, where he appears to be targeting victims randomly...or who happen to have the misfortune to come within his crosshairs..."

Declan had moved over to sit beside Stella as Ursula continued. "Speaking of the unsub, security camera footage near two different crime scenes indicates a serious person of interest as our chief suspect." She put the video images on a split screen. "Though the unsub's head is covered by a hood from the hoodie that's worn, along with dark clothing and dirty running shoes—we believe the suspect is a tall white or light-skinned Hispanic male with short dark hair, likely in his mid to late thirties or early forties. He appears to be in pretty good shape, based on body type and the way the unsub has been able to make haste in distancing himself from the scenes. Based on surveillance videos obtained from the vicinities where the murders occurred, we believe that the suspect may have been driving a dark SUV during his escape." Ursula took a breath and said keenly, "The task force will flush him out into the open, whatever it takes, and stop this madness..."

Declan was inclined to agree, even if they weren't there yet. He regarded Stella, who had been taking everything in, and said to her interestedly, "So, what are your thoughts?"

She met his gaze and responded contemplatively, "I have a few ideas, and I'm ready to share..."

"Have at it." He nodded, thinking again about the surge of electricity he felt when their palms touched earlier. "We'll be happy to take whatever you have to offer in trying to get the bead on our unsub."

"Okay," Stella said equably and rose to her feet.

THOUGH SHE HAD been in this situation before, Stella still had butterflies in her stomach as she stood at the podium. Was it truly a case of nerves? Or was it because she was there on behalf of Declan, whom she had spent the last three years trying to avoid, more or less? *I wonder if it was only my imagination when we shook hands and our skin touching somehow seemed to reverberate throughout my body as it had once before years ago?* she asked herself.

Stella broke away from the notion, absurd or not. She collected her thoughts for the moment at hand, deliberately avoiding Declan's steady gaze, as she went over mental notes and then said measuredly, "Though this perspective is subject to change once I delve deeper into the unsub's psyche—" which she hoped might not be necessary if they could nail the perp first "—based on what you've laid out on this Bends Lake Predator, my initial thoughts are that, as opposed to there being no rhyme or rhythm to the killings per se, I believe that, in fact, there is some rationale to what the unsub is doing…"

She took a short breath and went on, "For most serial killers, there is almost always a method to their madness, so to speak—even for what appears to be at face value random homicides—that may not be as discernible as we'd like in law enforcement. As it is, I worked on a similar type of serial killer case in Lansing, Michigan, last year where the victims were being gunned down, one by one in seemingly unrelated attacks…only to find out that there was something akin to an unorganized connection beneath the surface…"

I'd better get back to the point before I lose them, Stella told herself, glancing at Declan, who seemed glued to what was coming next. She swallowed and said evenly, "The fact that there have been three women and three men murdered is, in and of itself, indicative of a pattern of behavior. It tells me, for one, that the unsub is not gender specific in who he targets. Meaning that he is equally bent on killing women and men in order to satisfy his thirst for murder. This, of course, makes it difficult for law enforcement to zero in on one demographic for victimization to try and narrow down the killer's lane. Similarly," she needed to say, "the twenty plus age range of nineteen to forty for the victims means that the unsub is less interested in targeting a particular age group than he is in going after those who fit other situational characteristics—such as opportunity, location, time of day and a surefire getaway path—for the kills. This, again, complicates things when trying to narrow the focus for prevention and apprehension—"

Declan cut in as he asked her, "What's your take on the diverse racial and ethnic breakdown of the victims? Is there something to make of this in the unsub's head in terms of messaging or intent? Or is it entirely happenstance?" His voice rang with skepticism on that last note.

Stella didn't need much time to consider her answer, even if there were no absolutes in criminal profiling. She met Declan's eyes and responded coolly, "I seriously doubt that anything the unsub has done to this point is by chance. I believe that the variance in murders by race and ethnicity is not at all a reflection of some deep-seated prejudices against any groups in particular, when you consider the range of the victims' racial and ethnic background. My guess is that the choice to go after these individuals was meant more to confuse the authorities as to his motivation and keep them guessing, while making it more difficult to track down the unsub."

"Yeah, I feel the same way," Declan told her, giving a nod that they were in sync on this. "Which seems to fit in as well with the other range of victim characteristics…"

"True." Stella sighed and made sure she kept from slouching, a tendency she had at times, as she continued. "But that doesn't mean that the unsub's wide latitude and intentional guesswork in his killing ways makes him untouchable. No matter how deliberate his actions are, he's bound to make mistakes that will prove to be his undoing—similar to other smart serial killers like Albert Fish, Ted Bundy, John Wayne Gacy, Lonnie David Franklin Jr. and Richard Ramirez, to name a few. Most will not simply disappear into scary folklore, such as the infamous Whitechapel serial killer, Jack the Ripper.

"Now, in characterizing the Bends Lake Predator, beyond his physical appearance, I see him as a loner, but not necessarily alone. He may even be happily married with children, while still conducting his criminal activities without anyone in his inner circle being the wiser." She inhaled a breath. "Based upon the unsub's chosen method of killing, he's not one for wanting to get his hands dirty by committing the murders in more personal ways—such as by stabbing or strangling, which would make it easier to collect his DNA or fingerprints." Stella looked at her fellow FBI special agents, neither of whom she'd known when she worked at the KC field office herself. "The unsub would rather shoot his victims to death and get out of there as quickly as possible, while blending in with his surroundings. But his comfort with using a firearm also tells me that he could have honed his skills at a shooting range. Or could have a current or previous career in law enforcement or the military—or some other occupations that involve the use of firearms..."

Stella eyed Declan and couldn't tell if potentially implicating someone in law enforcement made him uneasy. Or not. Surely, he and others on the task force had already come to this same possibility, with catching the killer a top priority—wherever it took them.

She finished her initial assessment of the unsub by saying confidently, "I believe that the man you're looking for is a predatory killer—in that the murders are largely about the hunter preying upon his targets like a lion out for blood, as a recreational pursuit—and it appears, is just as bent on killing for hedonistic reasons, or in other words, a kill for the thrill mentality." Stella paused then gave a blunt warning, "Unless you can put a stop to the homicides, it is all but certain that they will continue for the reasons stated."

She left the podium on that note, knowing that she had given them food for thought as part of the overall investigation. It would fall upon Declan and the teams' collective laps to use this to paint a better portrait of the unsub as the hunt to capture him went on.

Chapter Three

"You did a great job in giving us a pretty good profile of the unsub," Declan told Stella as he drove her back to the hotel. He added silently, *and that's an understatement for how excellent an analysis it was.*

"Did you expect otherwise?" she asked, glancing at him.

He chuckled. "Not in the slightest. You obviously know your stuff, which is why I asked for you in particular, leaving nothing to chance in getting someone from the Bureau to size up the perp we're after." *And maybe there was another reason for wanting you back in Bends Lake—to try and repair our damaged relationship, if at all possible*, Declan told himself behind the wheel. But this probably wasn't the best time to bring that up.

"Just checking."

"And I'm happy to reassure you that we appreciate your input," he offered. None more than himself if it helped this case be solved as quickly as possible.

After a moment or two, Stella asked him tentatively, "So, what did you think about the possibility that the unsub could be a former or present member of law enforcement—present company excluded?"

"Hmm." Declan mused, his gaze fixed on the road.

He had considered this avenue himself, even if it pained him to think that the serial killer could be someone from among their ranks. "Well, honestly, I would've been surprised if you hadn't tossed that one out there to chew on."

"Seriously?" She angled her face. "I didn't want to step on any toes, but between the gunshot deaths and the relative ease on the unsub's part in avoiding certain roadblocks to his freedom, such as forensic evidence and other solid leads, it's kind of hard not to contemplate that the Bends Lake Predator could work in an occupation with enough know-how to evade detection up to this point."

"I don't disagree with you," Declan told her sincerely. "Trust me when I say that everyone on the task force is committed to finding the unsub, whoever he is, including if he carries a badge and firearm. That being said, we have no indication, thus far, that the perp is a member of law enforcement—in spite of the use by some of Springfield Armory 1911 Ronin Operator 9 mm pistols, on and off the job. But until the unsub is behind bars, I'll always keep an open mind. Even if my gut tells me that the killer is not one of us…"

"So long as your mind remains open, that's fine by me," Stella said. "My assessment as a criminal profiler is to be as inclusive as possible when characterizing the unsub. I don't mean to step on any toes."

"You haven't." Declan faced her with a reassuring grin. "It's all good. Keep doing your job and let the chips fall where they may."

"All right." She ran a hand through her hair. "If I come up with anything else that I believe might be helpful to the investigation, I'll be sure to let you know—either here or when I'm back in Detroit, assuming you haven't cracked the case by then."

In more ways than he wanted to admit, Declan found himself hoping she would stick around for a while—maybe even after the investigation had ended—if only to have an opportunity to reconnect. Or was she even open to the possibility of such on a more personal level?

After they reached the hotel, Declan felt it incumbent upon himself to offer her a more comfortable place to reside than her present accommodations. "Just want to put out there that the offer still stands, if you want to come to the house and chill—"

Stella seemed to consider the notion for what it was worth, before retreating, as she replied, "I'll stick it out here, but thanks, again…" She favored him with a half-hearted smile—or was it a smirk—before getting out of the car. "See you later," she said simply and closed the door.

Declan watched her walk away and couldn't help but wonder if they had taken two steps backward for every step forward. Or was he overanalyzing this? He owed it to her and Elise to not jump the gun when trying to sort out his feelings for Stella. Or wonder what hers were for him at this stage.

He drove off, knowing that there was still a murder investigation that commanded his attention. Even if he found himself wanting to spend time with Stella, getting to know her all over again. Never mind that it took two to tango, and she didn't seem that inclined to accompany him to this dance.

JUST TALK TO HIM, the voice in Stella's head told her, as she glanced over her shoulder while Declan was driving away. Yes, there was still a wall due to circumstances that neither of them had prepared for. But to evade getting to the root of it—like a cavity—was probably not a good idea. After all, wasn't confronting Declan at least part of the reason why she agreed to return to Bends Lake?

Inside her room, Stella finished unpacking, as if she planned to be there for a while, and then went to grab a bite to eat at the hotel's restaurant, before returning to the room to map out her schedule for providing more insight on the serial killer to the task force and then taking some personal time to reflect on her return home.

An hour later, Stella had changed into a purple tank top, blue shorts and white athletic sneakers and was using the elliptical exercise machine in the hotel's fitness center. She loved working her body to stay fit. This included jogging, swimming and karate, the latter having come in handy for self-defense, both on and off the job, from time to time.

Afterward, she hopped in her car and drove around, reacclimating herself to Bends Lake, while thinking about Elise and how everything that seemed so right in her life went so wrong in a split second. At least she had been given a taste of happiness, riding it like a prized stallion for as long as she was allowed to before disaster struck.

Much like my own life, when I thought I had it all— until it was taken away from me, Stella told herself mused about her short romance with Declan before he turned his attention elsewhere, breaking her heart in the process.

What's done is done, she thought, refusing to wallow in self-pity. Declan made his choice in Elise, and Stella felt that they both had to live with it, having moved on with their lives with her sister dead and buried.

She headed back to the hotel room, wanting to go over the file that Declan had sent her on the Bends Lake Predator, in case she missed something that might require an adjustment in her characterization of the unsub.

Ursula Liebert would not have wished what the parents of Peggy Elizondo were going through on her worst enemy. Having seen up close and personal the devastation of losing a family member to gunfire when her brother Gabriel was shot to death during an armed robbery more than a decade ago, Ursula knew all too well what Naveen and Julianne Elizondo would have to deal with. They were forced to reconcile themselves with the reality that Peggy was gone and never coming back. The fact that the young schoolteacher's death was a senseless act of violence, perpetrated by a serial killer, made it all the more painful.

Ursula was behind the wheel of her official vehicle, a Chevrolet Malibu, while en route to the Winstone Apartments on Fennkel Road, where Peggy lived. Her parents had come to collect Peggy's things. The medical examiner had released the victim's body to the local mortuary, from which her parents planned to bring her back to Eagle Pass, Texas, for a proper burial.

I can only hope that we find the unsub responsible for Peggy's death and give her folks some peace of mind, Ursula told herself, knowing that the stakes grew higher with each death attributed to the Bends Lake Predator. It was up to her and Declan, along with the rest of the task force, including its newest additions from the FBI, to capture the perp before there was more bloodshed, if possible.

Having Declan's sister-in-law, Stella Bailey, on hand could only be a plus to the investigation. Ursula had actually read one of her books on criminal profiling and got a lot out of it. Maybe the pretty behavioral analyst's interesting interpretation of the man they were after could actually lead to uncovering his identity and his subsequent arrest. Declan, who was obviously fond of his late wife's sister, even if he tried hard not to show it too much, certainly seemed to think so.

Ursula was fully on board with whatever steps they took to achieve their objectives. She pulled into the parking lot and left the vehicle before heading to Peggy's third-floor apartment to convey more sympathies to her parents. And provide an update on the status of the case, though knowing full well that there wasn't much more to tell.

Other than that, sadly, the unsub was still very much at large.

DECLAN SAT ON the bench at Rory's Gym on Quail Road, lifting weights to maintain his muscles as a prelude to running on the treadmill, one of his exercise routines before or after work or on the weekends. It was a good way to get the heart pumping and stay in shape.

Not to mention occupy his thoughts for a bit while the stress and strain of an active murder investigation was underway. Then there was seeing Stella again, bringing up old memories as if they were only yesterday. Instead of preceding his relationship with her sister.

We can't go back, Declan told himself as he stepped

onto the treadmill in his workout clothes of a T-shirt, sweat shorts and training sneakers. Could they? He would settle for just having Stella back in his life as a friend. And someone with whom he shared a painful loss.

Half an hour later, after showering and changing his clothes in the locker room, Declan said goodbye to a couple of others in law enforcement and headed out the door.

It took ten minutes before he was pulling up to his circular driveway on Rochel Lane. He and Elise had purchased the century-old, renovated, two-story farmhouse with four bedrooms and three bathrooms, sitting on four acres of rural land that offered a great view of the Cheyenne Bottoms wetland, during their first year of marriage. They believed it would be a great place to settle down and raise a family. Declan winced at the thought that this was no longer possible, with Elise in a grave.

Exiting the car, he made his way inside the house and took in the place with its old-school charm, rich hickory architecture and modern updates that brought it into the current century. This included a state-of-the-art security system, custom blinds for double-hung windows throughout, reclaimed hardwood flooring, high-end appliances, a great room, dining room and gourmet kitchen with a rustic island and glazed porcelain tile. There was an eclectic mix of traditional and retro furniture.

Upstairs were all four spacious, well-appointed bedrooms, one of which had been converted into a home office. Aside from the primary suite with an en suite bathroom, there were two other rooms for guests that had their own private bathrooms. One of the rooms, Declan imagined, had Stella's name on it, should she change her tune and decide to spend the balance of her stay in the house he and Elise had tried to make a home in Bends Lake.

After grabbing a frozen pepperoni-and-cheese pizza out of the freezer of the stainless-steel refrigerator, Declan put it inside the electric range oven before he headed up the spiral staircase. He put away his firearm and freshened up, then went back downstairs, got a bottle of beer from the fridge, opened it and took a sip as he waited for the pizza to cook.

Later, while sitting at the island on a solid wood stool eating, Declan found himself wishing Stella had taken him up on the offer to stay at the house. He could have used the company, feeling that the place was too big for one person, but believing it to be too good of an investment for now and into the future to sell it unwisely.

Still, it was tough being there right now, knowing that tomorrow would mark three years to the day that Elise died. Declan imagined that Stella was thinking the same thing—giving them both something to mourn, while trying their best to get on with their lives and whatever the future held.

THE NEXT DAY, Stella walked across the damp, well-manicured lawn of the Bends Lake Cemetery on Outon Lane till she came upon the gravesite of Elise. Cringing as she gazed at her sister's granite headstone, it pained Stella to think that someone so energetic and enthusiastic about the future she had planned with Declan could be taken away so cruelly and likely without Elise even knowing what hit her in the broadside collision.

It could just as easily have been me to die, had I been the one Declan chose to make a life with in marriage,

Stella told herself, fighting back tears. Her emotions were mixed at the prospect of having become his wife. Had she fought harder to keep Declan, it could not only have altered the course of history for herself—which could have meant an entirely different fate than what befell Elise—but could have prevented her sister from dying so young and being deprived of the long life she deserved.

When Stella heard some rustling behind her as someone was approaching, she turned around and saw Declan standing there. In his hands was a bouquet of crimson roses.

"Hey." His voice was solemn. "Had a feeling I might see you here."

Stella blinked. "I wanted to visit Elise's grave on the third anniversary of the day she died." She doubted she needed to explain this but did so anyway.

"Me too." He laid the flowers against her headstone. "I try to come as often as possible, whether Elise is aware of it on some level or not. Just seems like the right thing to do."

"I think she would like that," Stella told him honestly. It was a way to keep her sister's memory alive for the man she was wed to. For her own part, Stella kept Elise alive in her heart, even from afar. "It's still hard to believe Elise is no longer with us."

"Yeah, I feel the same way," Declan said, gazing at the gravesite. "She deserved so much better than to have it all end that way."

Stella concurred and told him so. She added mournfully, "Not a day goes by that I don't think of her." *Or what might have been had both of our lives taken a dif-*

ferent turn, she thought, glancing at the flowers and turning to Declan.

"Can we talk?" His eyes narrowed thoughtfully.

She cocked a brow and asked curiously, "You mean here…?"

"Actually, I was thinking more of a restaurant," he replied evenly. "Can I buy you lunch?"

Her first thought was to object, pulling away from him. But then she realized this was something that needed to happen—no matter how tough it could be for her. Or him, for that matter. Bottling up emotions was never a good thing. Even if she had managed to do so for the past three years, perhaps against her better judgment.

"All right," Stella told him tonelessly. "I'll follow you there."

He nodded and they both took one final look at Elise's grave in a united show of love and respect.

Chapter Four

Stella wasn't quite sure what to expect—including from herself—as she sat in the booth across from Declan at Teresa's Grill on East Maple Street. *Just hear him out*, she told herself, as Stella tried to concentrate on the menu. And allow Declan to hear what she had to say and go from there.

She settled on salmon cakes and a spinach salad and watched as Declan ordered the margherita flatbread, garlic braised short ribs and a side garden salad. Both went with black coffee and water.

After a moment or two, Declan sighed and said, "Let's just clear the air, if we can..." He tasted the coffee musingly as Stella waited with bated breath. "I'll start by saying what I probably should have a long time ago. If I had known when I met her that Elise Goldoni was your sister, I would never have started dating her, much less married her. But that knowledge didn't come till I had fallen head over heels for your sister—after things between you and I had ended..."

"And whose fault was that?" Stella challenged him, allowing her bitterness at essentially being dumped to overshadow her acknowledgment that their relationship was over when he met Elise, for better or, more likely, worse. "You didn't exactly fight for me…for us—"

Declan furrowed his brow. "I wasn't sure at the time that there was anything worth fighting for."

Her lashes fluttered. "Oh really?"

"Let me clarify that… I cared for you a great deal and wanted things to work out between us. But—" he halted his words, looking down and then back at her "—it seemed to me that you were just too dedicated to your career to want to be in a real relationship."

Stella spurted out, "And you weren't just as dedicated to your own career?" She refused to make this easy for him. Why should she? "That's pretty lame. Most people can actually have their careers and solid romances at the same time. It's called life. I was certainly ready and willing to try and meet you halfway." She clutched the coffee mug. "But you never gave us a chance…"

"If you want to know the truth, I guess I thought we were on the same page, more or less, with respect to where things stood between us," Declan muttered, jutting his chin.

Her eyes flashed hotly at him. "I think we were reading different books," she countered sarcastically. "I was never opposed to making compromises if it meant being in a stable relationship."

"Fair enough." Declan pursed his lips, sitting back. "I misread things, in sticking with that school of thought. My fault. As for the work ethic, you're absolutely right, I'm just as career driven as you are—if not more. I guess I didn't see things as clearly as I should have at the time in failing to look in the mirror at myself while judging you. I'm sorry." He took a long pause, staring at his coffee. "That's probably too little, too late—but I needed to get it out there anyway. You deserved better than what you got from me..." His voice dropped an octave. "Maybe Elise did too—"

Stella favored him with a straight stare. She hadn't seen that coming—him owning up to his role in their break up. In truth, she was probably every bit as responsible in not giving it her all to try and work things out.

But she was equally tuned in to his confession that he hadn't been everything that Elise had wanted as a husband. What exactly was he saying?

Before Stella could get to the root of it, the food was served.

Now Declan felt as though he was in the hot seat, having owned up to bowing out of their relationship, perhaps prematurely, when it seemed as if they were at a crossroads. Or, at the very least, not entirely on the same page as it related to what—and whom—they wanted out of life. Had he jumped the gun back then? Should he have stuck it out longer to see if they might have worked things out—thereby changing the course of both of their histories? Not to mention Elise's?

I can't undo what's been done, he told himself as they ate in silence. Decisions were always made, at every step of one's life, by doing what seemed best at the time. Should this be any different?

His thoughts turned to Elise. He could almost read Stella's mind speculating about his words regarding her sister deserving better than she got from him. Knowing he owed Stella an explanation, Declan held up slicing his knife into the tender short ribs and gazed across the table as he said, "About Elise—just so you know, I loved your sister and always wanted to do right by her." He stopped musingly, eyeing the coffee that had been refilled into his mug. "But, like you said, I was into my job, probably more than I should have been—too much. Maybe if I had worked less and spent more time with Elise, I might have been driving with her that day and somehow averted what happened—" Even after three long years, he could hardly bring himself to say the words: *car accident*.

Stella furrowed her brow as she used her fork to cut into a salmon cake and said insistently, "You can't blame yourself. The accident wasn't your fault, any more than it was mine. Elise was simply in the wrong place at the wrong time. No amount of second-guessing will ever change that."

"Maybe you're right," he conceded, nibbling on the margherita flatbread. "It's still hard not to, though. Elise should be here right now, living out her dreams."

"Yes, in an ideal world." Stella drew a thoughtful breath. "But she was able to make the most of the time she had. Being married to you made her happy, and Elise wouldn't have traded that for anything in the world." She paused again. "Neither would I, knowing how much you meant to her."

"Elise meant as much to me," Declan said sincerely. He was glad to see that Stella had been able to get past the bitterness of their own failed relationship to show sisterly love for Elise. That meant everything to him. And by extension, it told Declan that things were not as far apart between them as he'd feared. "I've missed having you in my life, Stella," he couldn't help but admit, knowing that they were friends first, before the romance followed.

"Me too," she surprised him by saying. "I think we both needed some time to reflect on everything before breaking the ice—"

"You're right." Declan didn't dare say he wished they had broken the ice sooner, settling for the moment at hand. He ate some of his salad and watched as she chewed a piece of salmon cake, then asked out of curiosity—or perhaps it was more than that, "So, are you seeing anyone these days…?"

Stella finished eating and replied succinctly, "No." She met his eyes. "But before you assume it's a work issue—it's not. More like the right person simply hasn't come along. I'm not interested in putting myself out there and falling flat on my face…"

Declan felt a pang in his chest while wondering if that was a backhanded way of getting back at him for short-circuiting things between them prematurely. Or was he misinterpreting her words for all the wrong reasons? "That's perfectly understandable," he told her, tasting his water.

"What about you?" she asked him, peering across the table. "Anyone special in your life?"

Declan lowered his chin. "Not since Elise," he answered candidly.

"It's been three years." Stella drew a sharp breath. "My sister would not fault you for moving on with your life. Actually, knowing her as I did, she would have insisted upon it—including in the romance department."

He didn't doubt that for one moment, as Elise was the type of loving person who encouraged him to live life to the fullest—even if it now meant finding that special someone to share his life with. Ironically, Elise wished too that would find her true soulmate one day.

Declan gave her a crooked grin and said evenly, "I'll keep that in mind."

She smiled. "You should."

"I will," he promised. "Like you, though, as soon as that right person comes into my viewfinder, I'll know and can act accordingly, if we're in sync—"

Even in saying this, he couldn't help but wonder, if things had worked out differently with Stella, whether she might well have been a perfect fit into that puzzle of his life and times. Had that time come and gone?

Or perhaps, in some strange way, the universe had found a way to reunite them—with the possibilities of moving forward in the palms of their hands?

STELLA CHECKED IN with her parents after going back to the hotel, knowing that they were sorrowful on the third anniversary of Elise's death.

As Ngozi and Lester Bailey appeared on the screen of her cell phone, both in their sixties, Stella offered them a soft smile, having always had their support in both her personal and professional lives, in good times and bad. Just as had been true for Elise with their parents.

"Hey," Stella said to them in an even tone.

Her father, sporting a salt-and-pepper quiff hairstyle, pushed up the square glasses over his blue eyes and said animatedly, "Hi, honey."

Her mother, still as beautiful as Stella remembered from when she was a little girl, with dark brown eyes and long, straight gray hair with the ends curled, asked carefully, "How's it going there in Bends Lake?"

"So far, so good," Stella answered truthfully, as she pondered the get-together with Declan and smoothing out unresolved issues. "I'm doing what was asked of me by the Bureau and waiting to see what happens."

"I hope your input will help them find the person they're after," Ngozi said.

"Me too." Stella looked at their faces before saying, "I went to Elise's gravesite today." She took a reflective breath. "I just miss her so much."

"I know you do." Ngozi's eyes watered. "She's always with us."

Stella felt her own eyes moisten. "I ran into Declan there—"

"How's he doing?" Lester asked equably.

"He's hanging in there," Stella answered. "Just trying to get on with his life as best as possible."

"We all are," her mother said, pausing. "So glad that you two have had a chance to talk. Elise would've wanted that."

"I know," Stella conceded. She and Declan had come clean with Elise about their prior involvement. Her sister, while shocked, had taken it in stride, as Elise believed that what had been bad for them had opened the door for her and Declan to come together. Even if initially unnerved at the prospect, Stella had come to realize deep down that she and Declan hadn't been ready to move ahead with their relationship. Elise, on the other hand, had come into Declan's life at the right time, and vice versa, and was entitled to run with it and find the happiness he gave her till the very end.

It was hardly anything that Stella could begrudge either of them, and she never would. She was glad that the tension in the air had softened between her and Declan. Maybe there was still a chance that as two single adults there might be something there for them to explore down the line.

After ending the call with her parents, Stella grabbed a bottle of water from the mini fridge. She drank a generous amount before settling onto the mid-century modern sofa with her laptop to catch up on some work.

BENDS LAKE POLICE OFFICER Jeremy Ponte was sitting in his Tesla Model Y patrol car on the side of the road, on the lookout for reckless speeders. In the ideal world, he would be sitting on the beach in Maui, Hawaii, retired and sipping pineapple margaritas with his girlfriend, Cassidy. But the real world required that, at thirty-six, he still needed to make a living to be able to afford the lifestyle and luxuries that made her happy—perfectly reasonable as they were.

His train of thought was interrupted when dispatch reported an armed robbery at a convenience store on Allen Street. The unsub was described as a dark-haired, white male in his thirties who fled the scene in a blue Buick Enclave SUV.

With the crime scene only a few blocks away, Jeremy was more than ready to do his part to try and track down the culprit. That became a bit easier when a traffic surveillance camera spotted a vehicle matching the description of the getaway car and a license plate reader was able to capture the plate number. More importantly, it appeared to be headed his way.

No sooner had that thought entered his bald head when Jeremy's gray eyes watched as the Buick Enclave with the right license plate number whizzed by him on Fortlene Road like its occupant was late for a party. After activating his police lights, he took off in full pursuit of the suspect while radioing for backup. He would try and cut off the vehicle before it could blend in with traffic.

Feeling an adrenaline rush, Jeremy put on some speed, not wanting to let the perp out of his sight. Unfortunately, the armed robbery suspect seemed to have a different idea, as he sped up in a blatant attempt at getting away.

The song and dance between them came to a screeching halt, quite literally, as Jeremy watched the unsub's vehicle spin out of control during a sharp turn onto Ellington Road and then hit a barrier in a construction zone. The driver managed to stagger out of the car, clearly dazed.

Jeremy, with a six-five sturdy frame, was quick to exit the patrol car. After turning on his body-worn camera and removing the Glock 22 .40 S&W service pistol from his tactical holster, he approached the suspect, just as a firearm fell out of the man's zip-up jacket.

Kicking what he recognized as a Springfield Armory 1911 Ronin Operator 9 mm handgun away from the suspect, Jeremy promptly placed him under arrest for speeding and other traffic-related violations, for starters.

DECLAN SAT IN a wooden chair at a metal table across from the armed robbery suspect in an interrogation room at the Bends Lake Police Department on Sorenten Street. Identified as thirty-five-year-old Todd Kavanaugh, he was slender with dark hair in a cropped cut and blue eyes. He also had a criminal record that included robbery and a DUI.

Under normal circumstances, Declan might have left this to the local law enforcement. But his interest in the suspect was piqued as a result of the firearm that fell from his pocket after crashing the stolen vehicle he was driving during a police chase, while coming away from it disoriented but otherwise uninjured.

The Springfield Armory 1911 Ronin Operator 9 mm pistol was the same type of handgun used to commit six homicides by the unsub known as the Bends Lake Predator.

Could this be the murder weapon?

We'll know soon enough, Declan thought as he sized up the robbery suspect, wondering if he might be a serial killer as well. His pistol was being examined by the KBI's Firearm and Toolmark Section to determine if the fired bullets and spent cartridge cases recovered could be linked to the handgun used by the Bends Lake Predator to take out six individuals.

After staring at the suspect for a long moment, who was identified by both the victim and surveillance video, Declan said evenly, "Armed robbery is a serious offense in Kansas, which I'm sure you know, having been down this road before. Yet, here you are…facing some heavy time behind bars."

Kavanaugh, who had yet to lawyer up, giving Declan free rein to interrogate him, wrinkled his nose and muttered defiantly, "I guess I'll just have to deal with it."

"I guess you will," Declan shot back. "Could be that this is the least of your problems…" He sat back, glaring at the suspect in feeling him out. "Tell me about the

9 mm handgun you used to rob the Brakers Store on Allen Street?"

Kavanaugh hunched his shoulders. "What's there to tell?"

Declan pursed his lips. "For starters, you might want to tell me where you got the gun—" which was already found to be unregistered and possessed illegally by the suspect "—and, more importantly, what other crimes were committed with the firearm." *We know that it had been fired more than once*, Declan told himself.

"I used it to rob a couple of other stores, okay?" Kavanaugh responded tartly. "I borrowed the gun from a friend."

"Does the friend have a name?" Declan pressed and thought, *If one isn't guilty of committing multiple murders, maybe the other is.*

Kavanaugh waited a beat before responding, "Lenny Vergara." He sighed. "He has nothing to do with this—"

"He has everything to do with it," Declan begged to differ. "Besides the gun being an illegal weapon and used in the commission of a serious crime, a Springfield Armory 1911 Ronin Operator 9 mm pistol just like it has been used by a serial killer in Bends Lake in recent months. I wonder if you or this Lenny Vergara know anything about that...?"

Kavanaugh looked nervous as he licked his lips and insisted, "Hey, I never killed anyone..." He hesitated. "I can't speak for Lenny."

"Guess he'll have to speak for himself." Declan peered at the suspect and was about to grill him further on this, when Ursula entered the room.

She glanced at Kavanaugh and said to Declan tonelessly, "Can I have a word?"

He nodded, got to his feet and told the suspect, "Be right back."

In the hall, Ursula made a face and said, "We got the results back on the 9 mm handgun Kavanaugh possessed."

"And?" Declan asked her.

"It wasn't a match," she said matter-of-factly. "This isn't the same weapon that was used by the Bends Lake Predator to shoot to death six people."

Declan jutted his chin in hearing the not-so-shocking news. "It was worth a try," he said soberly. "Unfortunately, Kavanaugh won't be walking away, as there are several other charges he'll have to answer to."

"Right." Ursula met his eyes. "In the meantime, we'll keep at this, till we find our man."

"And we will," Declan told her with conviction, trying to ignore the disappointment that Todd Kavanaugh wasn't the culprit.

Chapter Five

That evening, Stella sat on a faux-leather stool at Hedy's Club, a bar on Sixth Street. Around the lounge table were Declan and Ursula, along with FBI special agents Keene Haverstock and Arielle Mendoza. They were sharing a pitcher of beer and a large bowl of assorted nuts.

After listening to the discussion about armed robbery suspect Todd Kavanaugh, who turned out not to be the unsub they were seeking to track down, Stella weighed in by pointing out perceptively, "I could have told you that Kavanaugh wasn't our serial killer." She had watched the suspect being interrogated in another room but was only there to observe, unless her opinion had been sought.

"Oh really?" Declan cocked a brow amusingly and tasted his beer. "What did you see or not see in Kavanaugh?"

"Well, if you truly want to know, I could tell by his demeanor and the way he responded to your questions that being an armed robber and a violent serial killer were not one and the same in this instance. That being said, the charges against the suspect are serious," Stella had to say, as she scooped up a few nuts. "Then there was the fact that the one who Kavanaugh claimed actually owned the gun could well have turned out to be the perp—had the Firearm and Toolmark Section not proven otherwise in eliminating it as the Bends Lake Predator's Springfield Armory 1911 Ronin Operator 9 mm pistol. So, in other words, you were certainly right to check out Kavanaugh in the investigation, considering."

Declan feigned a sigh of relief. "I feel a lot better now." He chuckled and lost it on a dime. "Unfortunately, that doesn't bring us any closer to nailing the serial killer perp."

"I disagree," Ursula said, holding her mug. "Confiscating Kavanaugh's Ronin Operator pistol gives us one less illegal firearm on the streets while also eliminating one that might've belonged to the unsub."

Arielle grabbed a handful of nuts and said, "That's true. Makes our job a little easier in the process of trying to track down as many registered as well as unregistered handguns that fit the bill."

"Okay, I stand corrected." Declan laughed. "We're making progress, slowly but surely."

Keene's gray eyes lit up as he drank beer, then said after belching, "All of us from the Bureau are happy to lend a hand in catching the unsub—however long it takes." He gazed at Stella. "Having a top profiler come in to assist is huge."

"I couldn't agree more," Declan said, a lift in his voice. "Stella definitely knows her stuff. Always has."

Stella blushed, flattered by the compliment, especially coming from him. She sipped her beer and said, "Look who's talking. Must be something about being familial. Or maybe it's in the water—infecting us all," she added merrily, to try and keep it from sounding too personal. Even if it felt that way.

Unbeknownst to them, at a nearby table in the bar sat the Bends Lake Predator, who was coolly nursing a gin and tonic. Caught up in his own dark thoughts, he relished having the power of life and death—all at his whim. He wondered who would be next to take a bullet—make that a few bullets—from his reliable Springfield Armory 1911 Ronin Operator 9 mm pistol. He pretended that it could be anyone in there at the moment.

Maybe the guy with the uneven black hair at the table over there.

Or perhaps the good-looking biracial woman with long dark hair who the man was talking to.

Or even one of the other three people who shared their table.

He couldn't quite make out what they were talking about. And was only mildly curious.

He thought the pretty, dark-haired woman had looked his way. Or was it only his imagination?

Either way, he quickly shifted his own gaze. The last thing he wanted was to attract unwanted attention.

Not when he needed to remain anonymous in order to continue carrying out the executions that fueled his dark desires, separating somewhat from the other part of his life that required he conform to societal rules, to one degree or another.

Finishing off his drink, he refrained from having one more for the road.

The Bends Lake Predator ran a hand through his hair and stood up, casually walking away and in the opposite direction from the group of five still seated around the table talking shop.

As Declan drove Stella back to the hotel, he found himself wishing they could go to his house instead. Maybe have a nightcap and just talk. That was perhaps what he missed most in their earlier time together—feeling comfortable enough with each other to talk about whatever came to mind.

Or at least till the time arose that neither of them cared to talk much about what they truly wanted out of life and if it was possible to achieve it together.

I'll have to put much of the blame on myself, he truly believed, part of him wishing they could go back in time for a redo. With the other part knowing that, in so doing, he would be taking away the short period of happiness he and Elise had given each other.

Declan glanced at Stella and wondered what was going on inside her head. Apart from the insight she had displayed by correctly profiling Todd Kavanaugh, which could only serve them well when they finally caught up to the serial killer at large. She was probably thinking about how soon she could get out of Bends Lake and return to the life she had created for herself in Detroit. The thought of losing her once more was a hard pill to swallow.

He broke the silence by saying candidly, "Looks like we still have our hands full with the Bends Lake Predator investigation."

"What else is new?" Stella turned to him. "Let's face it, Declan, you enjoy this sort of thing—even if it is serious business."

"When you put it that way..." He laughed.

She chuckled. "You said it, not me." Her hand brushed against his knee. "As it relates to your case, trust me when

I tell you that the perp is feeling the heat much more than you or I. Killers—especially serial killers—may present a deceptively cool and calm veneer, but they are quite the opposite inside and forced to constantly think and rethink what they are doing and just how long they can get away with it. You've got this, Declan—eventually."

"You're right," he told her, his level of confidence returning. "Particularly with your help—and the rest of the task force," Declan decided to add for her sake.

She smiled. "Duly noted."

When he pulled up to the hotel, Declan said, "Here we are."

"Thanks for the ride," she told him.

"Anytime." He meant this in every way.

After a long moment, Stella leaned into him and kissed his mouth. It was sweet and painfully short as she pulled back, touched her lips and uttered, "I probably shouldn't have done that. Sorry."

"Don't be," Declan came to her rescue, finding the kiss to be to his liking. He considered following her lead by initiating another kiss, but wouldn't press his luck. "It was nice," he told her nonetheless as flashes of history danced in his head.

Stella blushed. "Good night, Declan."

He grinned. "Good night."

After she exited the car, gave an awkward wave and headed toward the hotel, Declan watched for a moment or two before driving off, giving himself more possibilities to contemplate.

What was I thinking? Stella asked herself once she was back inside her hotel room. Wasn't making a move on

Declan—or maybe that was an exaggeration, kissing him—inappropriate on so many levels? Hadn't they been there and done that before, ending in disaster? Would it be any different this time around—even with Elise no longer there to come between them, through no fault of her own?

Long-distance relationships did not work, and Stella was not inclined to go down that road. Not even for old times' sake.

And seriously, how much had really changed in their lives? Both were still very much involved in their careers. Was there enough wiggle room in between to have a successful relationship?

There you go overthinking things, Stella scolded herself, as she started to undress. However she tried to interpret it, it was just a kiss and hardly that. And she didn't get the impression that Declan was put off in the least. She wasn't sure if that was an opening that was begging them to both walk through. Or merely a moment of weakness that they needed to avoid at all costs in the future.

After taking a shower and slipping into a pink silk chemise, Stella responded to some messages on her cell phone before heading to bed.

The last thought on her mind prior to falling asleep was, not too surprisingly, Declan Delgado.

THE NEXT DAY, Declan used some time off to get in a quick workout on an outdoor basketball court in his neighborhood on Jecklin Avenue. He enjoyed stepping away from his official duties by shooting some hoops with active local youth. It was a way to recharge the batteries and do what he could to try and keep them on the straight and narrow, rather than them steering off track and having to answer to him or other law enforcement down the line.

He was going one-on-one with a seventeen-year-old kid named Aurelio Valderrama. A Latino, like himself, Aurelio was two inches taller, in at least as good shape, with brown eyes and black hair that had a textured crop top and an undercut. He worked part-time at a local delicatessen when not attending classes at Bends Lake High School, where he was a junior. After graduation, his dream was to attend Declan's alma mater, Wichita State University.

Tossing the ball to him, Declan challenged, "Let's see what you've got!"

Aurelio laughed arrogantly. "Sure you wanna find out?"

"Probably not," Declan kidded as the ball was tossed back at him. He bounced it once, threw it to Aurelio and said seriously, "But I'll take my chances…"

With that, they went at it, trading baskets and fouls, while working up a good sweat. Declan had no problem keeping pace, even while secretly admiring his opponent's seemingly endless energy and deft moves on the court.

By the time it was over, though, Declan had prevailed by a point, while knowing it could easily have gone the other way had Aurelio's last jump shot not bounced in and out of the basket.

Still, Declan couldn't help but be boastful when saying, "Good game. Better luck next time."

Aurelio chuckled as he bounced the ball on the court. "I'm not the one who'll need the luck," he argued. "See you later…"

"Count on it," Declan told him and headed in the opposite direction, toward his house. He looked forward to getting another crack at the younger opponent, while expecting the same result.

After grabbing a bottle of water from the fridge and downing it in one long gulp, Declan thought about how empty the place seemed these days. He imagined that Stella could certainly fit the bill in addressing that issue with her presence. Even temporarily. But was that even realistic, given the missteps in their history and the current trajectories of their lives?

What was that old adage about hope springing eternal? Declan mused wistfully, pushing past the obvious obstacles to taking up with Stella again. Who knew what the future could hold, if the will and want were strong enough both ways?

He got cleaned up before going into his home office, where there was a walnut adjustable sit-and-stand workstation, mid-back faux-leather computer chair and large window overlooking the wetland. After sitting down, he went to his laptop to review the Bends Lake Predator case and where they were in the investigation.

STELLA DECIDED TO bypass the fitness center to go outside for some fresh air and a power walk through the nature trail. She was mindful that the serial killer on the loose tended to target victims who were by themselves, no matter the location or time of day. And though the odds were against being singled out by the unsub, to be on the safe side, she carried her Glock 19 pistol in a concealed carry holster beneath her black workout tank.

Having been near the top of her class in pistol marksmanship while training at the FBI Academy in Quantico, Virginia, Stella assured herself she could more than hold her own when encountering an armed assailant. Especially one who may be overconfident, allowing her to turn the tables when least expected.

Hopefully, it will never come to that, she told herself, having no desire to confront the perp, even in broad daylight. She would push that onto Declan and other law enforcement tasked with taking down the Bends Lake Predator.

After a cool down and good stretch, Stella walked back to the hotel. She was moping around in the lobby, while wondering if she should reconsider Declan's offer to have her spend her remaining time at the old farmhouse he and Elise purchased, when a female's voice called out to her, "Stella…is that you…?"

Turning to her left, Stella regarded an attractive, slender woman about her height and age, with bold aquamarine eyes and a long, wavy blond balayage hairstyle. She was dressed in casual clothing and slingback sandals.

As Stella strained for recognition, though there was some familiarity, the woman said, "It's Gayle Reese—we went to high school together…"

Studying her further, it came back to Stella. "Gayle," she uttered. Though they didn't exactly hang out with one another at Bends Lake High School, she did remember her now, them having been in some of the same classes and on the swim team. Stella recalled that she had brunette hair in high school. "How are you?"

"I'm good." Gayle's tone flattened, but then she gave Stella a hug. "Been a while."

Hugging her back, Stella said, "Yes, it has." She was

sure they hadn't seen each other since shortly after graduating and going their separate ways. Stella thought that she might have heard through the grapevine years ago that Gayle had run off with a guy she met for parts unknown. Had she moved back to Bends Lake? Or, like herself, was she only here for a visit? "Are you staying at the hotel?"

Gayle licked her lips. "I wish." She batted fake lashes. "I'm actually working at the gift shop."

"Really?"

"Yeah, for a couple of years now—or ever since I moved back to town from Atlanta, following my divorce."

"I see." Stella was saddened to hear about the divorce—something she never wanted to experience—but was glad to know that Gayle had apparently gotten back on her feet. "Sorry the marriage didn't work out," she offered sincerely.

"So am I. It happens." Gayle sighed. "I just wish I'd gotten out of a bad relationship sooner, but didn't have the courage to go there till it finally came upon me."

Stella offered in response, "You did what you needed to, when it was the right time."

"Yeah." Gayle ran fingers across her hair. "I take it that you're a guest at the hotel?"

"Yes," Stella answered evenly. "Just for a few days on business," she added, leaving it at that for the time being. "I'm living in Detroit right now."

"Nice." Gayle smiled briefly then furrowed her brow. "I heard about your sister—I'm so sorry..."

"Thanks for that." Stella flinched, as if it happened just yesterday. "It was hard to fathom this could have happened to Elise, but time has allowed me to come to terms with it."

"I'm glad to hear that." Gayle flashed her a thoughtful look. "Well, I'm just finishing up my break, so I better get back in there. Maybe we can catch up later—"

"I'd like that," Stella told her, even if she wasn't sure she would have much time for socializing. Maybe she would make the time, in trying to get back in touch with her roots, with Elise no longer around to bounce things off of. And Stella wasn't certain how much she could trust herself in rebuilding things with Declan that could stick, in spite of the familiar comfort zone that seemed to be drawing them closer to each other like magnets.

Chapter Six

Diane Wexler was into her third lap in the custom swimming pool of the multimillion-dollar home she shared with her husband of nearly twenty-five years, Kendall. It was her absolute favorite pastime—she could easily swim for hours—but was by no means the only joy of her life. Another bright spot was her daughter, Estelle, who, at twenty-one, was only beginning her journey in life and the craving for independence at that stage.

Estelle's path was much like her own when Diane had been a free spirit. Till she had to grow up and had to assume responsibilities and face realities that brought her to this point in time. Would she change some things if she could do it all over? Probably—okay, so yes, definitely—when looking at her mistakes squarely. But then, who wouldn't make the necessary modifications along the way if given a second chance?

No regrets, remember? Diane reminded herself, counting her blessings, all told. She emerged from the pool, her magenta one-piece swimsuit clinging to her shapely body like a second skin above long, lean legs. Though forty-one years old, she prided herself in often being able to pass for someone ten years younger.

She grabbed a beach towel from the patio wicker

chaise longue, used it to dry her face and soak up water from her long V-shaped layered blond hair, then headed across the flagstone walkway toward her two-story brick estate.

But before she could go inside, Diane was thrown off guard as her blue-green eyes caught sight of a male figure who emerged from the side of the house. He was wearing dark clothes and dark leather gloves. There was a gun in his hand.

As she tried to come to grips with the person and her familiarity with him—not to mention overcome the fear that threatened to engulf her like a blaze—the assailant fired a shot at Diane's rib cage, shattering it. The force propelled her backward toward the pool. Clutching her chest while assessing the damage and pain, she was shot again; this time it ripped through her stomach.

When the next bullet hit her directly in the face, Diane immediately lost consciousness, before she fell backward into the pool, her life over.

DECLAN GOT THE call about a woman found dead in a swimming pool by her housekeeper at a home on Lavador Lane. She had apparently been shot multiple times, grabbing the attention of the KBI as it related to their ongoing investigation.

While en route to the scene, accompanied by Ursula in the passenger seat, Declan remarked in an understatement, "Looks like our killer may be at it again—albeit in an interesting location, given his standard modus operandi..."

"Or it may not be the unsub's work at all this time," Ursula cautioned him thoughtfully. "Six months ago, the KBI came to this location after there was a reported domestic violence incident. The suspected victim was the wife, Diane Wexler, with her husband, a wealthy real estate investor, Kendall Wexler, thought to be the aggressor. But she refused to press charges and that was that. Whether things escalated into the current situation remains to be seen."

"Six months ago, huh?" Declan went back to how she began. "About the same time that the Bends Lake Predator started murdering people. Could be some symmetry there—"

"Possibly." Ursula gazed out the window. "We're about to find out."

"Or not," Declan said, leaving enough wiggle room to move in a different direction, if warranted. He glanced at her, museful. "So, when's the due date for your baby?"

"Our precious little girl should be making her way into the world on Halloween," she answered.

"Should be a real treat and no tricks," he said lightheartedly.

"Definitely." Ursula laughed. "Both Melody and I are counting down the days."

Declan smiled. "As you should."

"Hey, you'll get to experience the joy yourself someday, Delgado," she told him with confidence.

"Hope so." He wasn't so sure about that, but saw some light at the end of the tunnel as Declan pondered the prospects and whether or not Stella might fit into the equation.

They pulled up behind a patrol car outside the Wexler's estate, got out and then headed toward the two-story brick house as Declan took note of the white Lexus NX 350 and blue Volkswagen Jetta parked in the driveway.

The front door opened, and they were met by Bends Lake Police Officer Judith Hansen, a tall thirtysomething woman with short red hair. After Declan identified himself, flashing his badge, and Ursula did the same, Judith, whose uniform was wet, said solemnly, "The victim's been identified as Diane Wexler by her housekeeper, Rhonda Kishi, who discovered her body in the pool shortly after showing up for work. According to her, the victim swam daily in the afternoon—which would indicate that she hadn't been dead for long."

Declan angled his face and said, while feeling bad for both the victim and housekeeper, "Was there anyone else at the house when you arrived?" His first thought was the husband.

"No one that I saw," the officer answered, adding, "I went through the place after calling it in. The killer had vacated the premises—if the person entered the house at all. There was no sign of forced entry."

"Interesting," Declan said, scanning the place. This would suggest that the unsub had accessed the swimming pool area from outside the house—and thus would have been privy to perhaps both the victim's routine and point of entry.

Ursula said to the officer, "Can you take us to the body?"

Judith nodded. "Right this way..."

They followed her across bamboo flooring and an expansive main level with expensive furnishings and lots of windows covered by plantation shutters, as Declan surveyed the layout and possible escape routes for a killer, till exiting out a sliding back door.

Near a pool house, Declan spotted a fiftysomething

woman with short dark hair wearing a housekeeper's uniform.

"I'll go talk to her," Ursula volunteered.

"Okay," Declan said, and turned toward the swimming pool.

Lying next to it was a white female, identified as Diane Wexler. She was wearing a swimsuit, her wet body covered in blood from what looked to be two gunshot wounds and her face shattered from a single bullet shot at close range.

"I pulled her out of the water and tried administering CPR—to no avail," Judith said, her lower lip quivering. "It was too late. She was already gone."

"You did what you could," Declan told her sympathetically. "Unfortunately, someone wanted to make sure that any such efforts would be in vain."

The Danver County medical examiner and KBI Crime Scene Response Team arrived and began their respective duties in dealing with a homicide and the quest for assessments and gathering crucial evidence.

Declan and Ursula listened as the medical examiner, Aaron Wilson, grimaced in going through the motions in his preliminary thoughts on the deceased.

"Same old, same old," he indicated sadly while flexing his nitrile gloves. "The victim was shot twice in the chest at close range and was likely finished off with a shot to the face." His brow creased. "It looks as though the decedent never really had a chance."

"Not by the looks of it," Ursula agreed.

Just like the others, Declan told himself, as the early indicators were that this had the trademarks of their serial killer at work. Even if the circumstances demanded that they keep an open mind.

They heard some noise and then saw a tall and sturdy man in his early forties, with brown hair in a taper cut and blue eyes, step out of the house, wearing business casual clothing and black leather derby shoes. He rushed toward the victim, who was still being attended to, calling out her name in sorrow.

Declan stepped in front of him, stopping his advance in compromising a crime scene. "Are you the husband?"

"Yes, Kendall Wexler." He grimaced. "I got the call from Rhonda, saying to get home...that Diane had been shot—"

"She was," Declan said candidly, while not knowing if he was truly shocked or just playing the part of a grieving husband. "I'm afraid your wife is dead."

Wexler's shoulders slumped. "Who would do this?"

"I was hoping you might be able to help us with that." Declan made eye contact with Ursula and turned back to him. "Why don't we go inside?"

Wexler glanced at his wife's body and hesitated before nodding. Declan followed him and Ursula caught up, as they were both interested in what the man had to say.

Standing in the center of the open concept great room, Wexler ran a hand through his hair and said sharply, "I have no idea who would have done something like this."

That's what all abusive spouses say, Declan told himself sardonically. He peered at the suspect. "Did your wife have any enemies?" he had to ask.

"No, none that I'm aware of," Wexler responded tersely. "She was liked by everyone."

Except for at least one person, Declan thought, and

regarded the husband. "How were things in your marriage?"

Wexler's brows knitted. "What exactly are you asking?"

"Was your wife—or you, for that matter—involved romantically with anyone else?" Declan threw out bluntly.

"Absolutely not," Wexler insisted. "We were both faithful in our marriage."

Maybe you were and maybe you weren't, Declan thought, knowing that infidelity and homicidal tendencies often went hand in hand. "Had to ask," he told him laconically.

As Wexler took this in, Ursula asked pointedly, "Do you mind telling me where you were when you received the call concerning your wife?"

Wexler looked at her. "I was at my office on Wymore Road."

"Can anyone vouch for that?" she asked.

"My administrative assistant, Mollie Chenoweth," he answered matter-of-factly. "Mollie was the one who actually took the call initially and passed it on to me."

Declan regarded him and asked, "When did you get to the office?"

Wexler scowled. "I'm not sure I like your insinuation."

"Not insinuating anything—just yet," Declan retorted. "Your wife was murdered, and it's our job to investigate it. That begins with the person closest to her and with the best knowledge of the layout of the property—"

Wexler drew a breath. "I got there at nine o'clock," he asserted. "And never left the office till I learned what had happened."

"So you say." Ursula narrowed her eyes at him suspiciously. "Question—did you ever hit your wife again after the incident that happened six months ago?"

Wexler's head snapped back as if he had been punched. "That was all just a big misunderstanding," he argued. "Things weren't perfect between us, as with any marriage, but I've never hit Diane. And I sure as hell wouldn't have killed her!"

Declan kept the heat on, wanting to cover the bases, just in case he was trying to play them. "Mr. Wexler, do you own a firearm?"

Wexler batted his eyes. "Doesn't everyone in this day and age?"

"It wouldn't happen to be a Springfield Armory 1911 Ronin Operator 9 mm pistol, would it?" he asked him directly, knowing this would make him an automatic suspect in the Bends Lake Predator case.

Wexler shook his head and responded, "No, it's a Korth 2.75 inch Carry .38 Special, 357 Magnum, 9 mm Luger revolver. I keep it locked away in a safe. Diane didn't want a gun in the house at all, but I insisted upon it for our protection." Lines deepened on his forehead. "Little good that did."

Declan and Ursula exchanged glances, then she asked Wexler, "Does anyone else live at the house?"

"Only my daughter, Estelle," he replied, "when she's home. Right now, she's attending college at the University of Oxford in England."

"Good school," Ursula remarked.

"Yeah," Wexler concurred.

Declan knew that Ursula's husband had graduated from Oxford University, and both took pride in it. Having noted that the house had a security system, he asked Wexler, "I'd like to take a look at your surveillance video."

Wexler said agreeably, "You're free to. But you won't find anything there. When I heard what had happened, I accessed the security cameras from my cell phone. There was no one inside the house. The camera showing the pool area was turned off by Diane while she swam." He paused. "We don't have a camera on the perimeter, leading to a wooded area behind the house. I'm guessing that the intruder came in that way... See for yourself—"

Wexler removed the cell phone from the pocket of his pants and played the video for them, then handed the phone to Declan. He examined it alongside Ursula, and as Wexler had indicated, there was no movement inside the house, which seemed to rule out robbery as a motive. No footage either of the assailant by the pool or the property's perimeter. Was this by design? And was there any reason, in particular, to target this individual?

"We'll need to take a look at your security video from the last twenty-four hours from all vantage points," Declan told Wexler.

"Sure, no problem." He was handed back the phone. "Whatever you need. Whoever did this to Diane, I want you to catch them."

"We all want the same thing," Ursula made perfectly clear.

Declan said to him, "We'll need to see your firearm, for verification."

Wexler complied, handing over his Korth Carry Special revolver to Declan. Studying it while wearing a latex glove, it was obvious to him that it wasn't the handgun choice of their serial killer. But this did not necessarily exonerate Diane Wexler's spouse from being her killer.

When Wexler's alibi checked out, he was given free rein to contact his daughter and make arrangements for his wife's burial as the investigation continued.

Hours later, Stella was walking alongside Declan downtown on Sorenten Street, not far from the Bends Lake Police Department, as he gave her the scoop on the latest murder to rock the town.

"After initially entertaining the thought that the victim might have been killed by her husband, Kendall Wexler," Declan was saying, "the preliminary ballistics report on the shell casings found and bullets removed from Diane Wexler's body links them to the same Springfield Armory 1911 Ronin Operator 9 mm handgun used to shoot to death six others. Or, in other words, this is most likely the work of the Bends Lake Predator."

As Declan furrowed his brow, Stella said with sincerity, "I'm so sorry for the victim that she had to die this way."

"Yeah, me too." Declan brushed against her shoulder. "Especially considering that she left behind a college-age daughter to have to try and pick up the pieces, along with her father—to carry on with their lives."

It made Stella think about Elise and the children she never got to have. How might her sister have ever been able to cope with such a tragedy, had it befallen her in losing a child? *No doubt the same as I'd feel—and Declan*, Stella told herself. She turned to him and said, "Based on what you told me about the way things went down with the murder—including the lack of surveillance video of the unsub and his likely escape route—it's clear to me that this killing, above all others, was carefully planned. The killer must have known, or figured out, the layout of the property and also may have stalked the victim to know her routine before acting on his dark impulses and successfully vacating the premises."

Declan ran a hand along his jawline and said, "I was thinking the same thing. He definitely knew what he was doing in seemingly going against the grain of the random-like nature of the other murders. It's possible that he and Diane Wexler were acquainted, in one manner or another, and she somehow managed to get on his bad side."

"True. It's also possible that any perceived acquaintanceship was all in his head," Stella threw out, "and along with it, a snub in his mind that motivated him to pay her back by adding her to his list of victims—while maintaining as much of his modus operandi as possible, so there was no mistaking who was behind the attack."

Declan frowned. "Now that the unsub has potentially chosen to make his killings more personal in nature—though opportunistic homicide is still possible—it makes it a little more complicated in figuring him out."

"Serial murderers are always complicated, to one degree or another," Stella told him knowingly. "This one is no more or less complex. The unsub has proven to be clever enough that any moves he makes are likely calculated for his own devious purposes and perhaps to keep the authorities guessing. It never works, when all is said and done. His strengths will ultimately be the same dynamics that bring him down."

Declan nodded and favored her with a grin askance. "I like the way you think."

She smiled at the thought. "Do you now?"

"Yeah, always have." He stopped walking as they approached a food truck. "Hungry?"

"Yes, I think I could eat something," Stella told him, running a hand across her ponytail.

"Same here. What's your pleasure?"

She studied the menu on the truck and went with a grilled chicken wrap and watched as he ordered a Philly cheesesteak taco.

As they waited for the food to come, Stella's cell phone rang. She pulled it from the side pocket of her linen pants and saw that it was her boss, Valerie Izbicki.

"I need to get this," Stella told Declan.

"Go ahead," he said. "I'll bring you the wrap when it's ready."

"Okay." She stepped away from him and answered the call. "Hey."

Valerie responded, "Just wanted to check on you and see how things are going."

"They're going," Stella told her dryly. "Actually, the serial killer case is still alive and well. In fact, it seems that the unsub just added another victim to his number of homicides," she hated having to say.

"Hmm...that's not good," the assistant special agent in charge said. "I take it that you've weighed in on the unsub?"

"I have." Stella watched as Declan was paying for their food. "It's still a work in progress as the unsub appears to be changing some of his tactics. Of course, if I'm needed elsewhere..." She let the words trail off while hoping to remain in Bends Lake for a bit longer to continue to mend fences with Declan.

"No, stay put for now," Valerie told her. "Do what you need to and give them your expertise to help nail this killer."

"Thanks. I'll do my best," Stella promised her.

She responded, "Keep me posted."

"I will."

After Stella disconnected, she saw Declan standing there. He asked, "Everything all right?"

"Yeah," she told him. "I was just giving my boss an update on where things stand in the investigation."

Declan was thoughtful. "I see." He handed her the grilled chicken wrap. "Hope you'll be able to stick around a little longer. I was just starting to get comfortable seeing you again."

"Me too." Stella gazed at him. "Unfortunately, it can't last forever," she warned honestly. She immediately wanted to take back the words, knowing that her career choices were what split them up before. Was it inevitable that history would repeat itself?

"I know." Declan glanced at his Philly cheesesteak taco and met her eyes. "But that doesn't mean we can't make the most of every moment you're here."

"I agree." She bit into her wrap while thinking, *Too bad most of those moments will be spent investigating a serial murderer.* "On a lighter note, I ran into an old friend from high school at the hotel."

"Is that right?" He dug his teeth into the taco. "Is she here visiting too or…?"

"Actually, she works at the gift shop." Stella nibbled on the food. "We weren't really all that close in school. Still, it's a small world."

"Tell me about it," Declan said. "I've had my fair

share of encounters over the years that remind me just how small the world truly can be."

Stella smiled, while wondering if that comment was directed in part at their own unexpected reunion and what it could mean in the scheme of things. "True," she said thoughtfully.

Suddenly, Declan reached toward her with a napkin and said, "You've got some sauce there that needs a little cleanup."

He pressed the napkin to a corner of her mouth, causing Stella to blush. "Thanks."

"Don't worry about it."

"Neither should you," she tossed back at him when spotting a bit of cheese that had landed on his chin, which she took the liberty of wiping away with her finger and showing him.

Declan laughed. "Guess we're both messy eaters," he joked.

"I think it's more like we're keeping our priorities in order," she told him with a chuckle, bringing back vivid thoughts of this natural repartee between them once upon a time.

They finished eating and headed back to the police department.

THE BENDS LAKE PREDATOR drove around inconspicuously in his SUV. He wouldn't exactly say he was hunting for new victims. But then again, if the opportunity arose that landed the right person in his crosshairs, he wasn't the least bit afraid of acting upon it.

On the other hand, he took more of an interest in some people than others—making the kill even sweeter. Diane

Wexler came to mind. Their paths had crossed, and when she had rebuffed his attempts to kick things up a notch, it told him everything he needed to know about her. And it wasn't pretty.

His plan had been executed flawlessly. She barely knew what hit her. Unlike the others, he didn't have the luxury of stretching things out before it was time for her to die. Not when the housekeeper would show up at any moment, had he chosen to dillydally.

And so, he put the attractive woman of the house out of her misery, short and sweet—before getting the hell out of there.

Another triumph to relish as he contemplated the authorities scratching their heads in frustration over his ability to run rings around them and get away with it.

Too bad. So sad.

The Bends Lake Predator laughed hysterically, knowing the sounds were trapped inside his vehicle. He continued to drive while staying well within the speed limit. The last thing he needed was for the cops to pull him over and find that he was in possession of the Springfield Armory 1911 Ronin Operator 9 mm pistol he used to take seven lives.

But were that to happen, he was always ready. Having the advantage of being able to read their minds before they could read his thoughts was all he needed to get the jump on any unsuspecting cop who got in his way.

Which happened to be equally true for anyone he encountered who was a step slower than him, for his better and their worse.

Chapter Seven

The next afternoon, Declan was in his KBI office, analyzing the autopsy report on Diane Wexler. It confirmed what he suspected and had been posited by Aaron Wilson. The victim died from a point-blank gunshot wound to her face, with two shots to the body contributing to the death—occurring before she fell into the swimming pool. Not surprisingly, the death was listed as a homicide.

Before he could chalk this up as the seventh murder committed by the Bends Lake Predator, Declan got on the phone with the forensic science lab's Firearm and Toolmark Section, where the spent shell casings and bullets removed from the victim were being analyzed.

He was connected to Josephine Okamura, a forensic scientist, to get the official word on the submissions to the evidence control center, after the preliminary findings.

Declan asked, "What's the scoop on the ballistics?"

Josephine, who had been with the KBI for the past decade, responded affirmatively, "It's a match. The recovered shell casings, bullets and bullet fragments definitely fit together and came from the same Springfield Armory 1911 Ronin Operator 9 mm pistol."

"Just as I thought," Declan told her.

"Now if we can get our hands on the weapon itself and positively link it with the ammo…"

"We can find the unsub and solve the case," he finished for her.

"Exactly," Josephine expressed.

Declan could not agree more. The trick was to make this happen as soon as possible and try to save more lives in the process. He disconnected and headed out the door to brief the field investigation division's special agent in charge, Kimberly Ullerich.

Stepping inside her corner office, he saw that she was on the phone while sitting on the edge of her walnut desk. In her early fifties, the slender Kimberly had strawberry blond hair in a cheekbone-skimming bob and was wearing oval glasses over blue eyes.

When she disconnected, Declan wasted no time in providing an update on the serial killer investigation. He finished with "We're going at this from every angle—till we hit pay dirt in bringing in the unsub…"

"That's good." Kimberly nodded, but her mind was clearly elsewhere. "I know you and the team will get it done. At the moment, though, we have a more pressing issue on our plate…"

"What is it?" Declan was attentive.

"We just got a report of a young child being abducted by her own mother. The estranged father had full custody of the eight-year-old girl." Kimberly frowned. "If this is as it seems, we need to find her before something bad happens that no one can undo—"

"Got it," Declan said, as he pondered the worst-case scenarios that no custodial parent should ever have to go through. His current case, unsettling as it was, could be put on hold just long enough to help bring this girl home.

STELLA SAT IN the coffee shop across from Gayle as both sipped black coffees. They spoke about their high school years and in general terms about nothing in particular.

"So, are you still swimming?" Stella asked curiously, even as a sad thought danced in her head of Diane Wexler being pulled out of a pool.

"Yeah, I try to swim in Lake Bends whenever I have the time and the weather's nice," Gayle answered. "How about you?"

"Yes, I still swim every chance I get." Stella glanced at her coffee, conceding that time wasn't always on her side for the pastime, with the constant demands of her job occupying her seemingly nonstop.

Gayle regarded her and asked inquisitively, "What do you do for a living?"

Stella waited a beat and then answered evenly, "I'm a special agent and profiler for the FBI." *That usually throws people for a loop, for whatever reason*, she told herself.

"Seriously?" Gayle's eyes popped wide. "I know we lost touch a long time ago, but I seem to recall you once expressing an interest in becoming a writer—"

Stella had to laugh. "Actually, I'm a writer too."

"Really?"

She told Gayle about her books on criminal profiling and added that she had also written some articles in leading journals. Stella even admitted to harboring a secret wish to try her hand one day at writing a novel—perhaps a romance or crime thriller.

"I have aspirations of my own," Gayle told her, tasting the coffee. "One of these days, I'd like to open my own shop—selling antiques and collectibles..."

"I say go for it, when the opportunity presents itself," Stella encouraged her, believing everyone should follow their dreams, if possible. Before fate ever had a chance to deal a fatal blow.

"Is there anyone in your life these days?" Gayle eyed her, seeming to take note that there was no ring on Stella's finger. "Or are you going solo, as I am right now, while I focus on myself for a change...?"

Stella immediately thought of Declan and their rekindled camaraderie. Wasn't exactly a romance, but did give her hope that there was still a place in her life for a real relationship. "Nothing to report at the moment," she said ambiguously. "Right now, there's no one I can say is in my life where we're both able and willing to look at the big picture."

Gayle lifted the mug to her lips and said philosophically, "Whatever will be, will be, for both of us..."

"I agree." Stella brought up her own mug and drank from it thoughtfully. When her cell phone rang, she lifted it from the pocket of her knit trousers and saw that the caller was Declan. "I need to get this," she told Gayle, who nodded in understanding.

After Stella addressed him, Declan said in a serious tone, "There's been a reported parental abduction. I'm heading over to the house of the father, who had full custody of the girl who was apparently taken unlawfully by her mother—his estranged wife. I was hoping you'd like to come along and assess what we might be up against in bringing the child home safely."

"Of course," Stella readily agreed. "Whatever I can do to help."

"Great. I can pick you up in ten minutes—if that's okay?"

"It is. I'll see you then." She disconnected and then told Gayle, "Something's come up. Have to go."

"I understand," Gayle said. "My break is just about over anyway."

They both stood and Stella told her smilingly, "Thanks for the coffee."

"Thank you for the company," Gayle responded. "It was fun reminiscing, and more."

"Same here." Stella met her eyes affably. "Catch you later."

Leaving the coffee shop, where they parted ways, Stella raced to her room for a quick refresh and was back downstairs. She waited outside for Declan to arrive, while hoping that the alleged child abduction could end peacefully.

"MAYBE THIS WAS just a simple misunderstanding," Stella tossed out from the passenger seat. "Where it concerns stressful matters of marital separation, oftentimes the parent who has custody can overreact if the other parent's visitation hours are off by even the slightest."

"That's not how I'm reading this," Declan responded from behind the wheel of his Chevrolet Malibu. He considered the Kansas laws pertaining to parental kidnapping that applied to children under the age of sixteen who were taken away or enticed to leave by a noncustodial parent and held or concealed from the custodial parent in the process. "From what I understand, the girl was apparently taken without the permission of her father, who was concerned enough for her safety to report it."

"Okay, so maybe I was being overly optimistic and idealistic in thinking in terms of the importance of the nuclear family and finding ways to keep it intact." Stella drew a breath. "Obviously, that's not always possible in the real world—especially when children are involved, and one parent or the other uses them as leverage, as a means to an end."

"We'll see which way the pendulum swings here and act accordingly."

For his part, Declan couldn't imagine exploiting his own child or children to save a marriage. Or as some kind of retaliation for a relationship turned sour. He knew that Stella, who would make a great mother, felt the same way. All they needed was to find it in themselves to go down that road of parenthood and all it stood for, even if they had to do that with different partners.

They arrived at a sprawling cattle ranch on Praglin Street on the outskirts of Bends Lake. Parked outside the two-story main house was a black Ford Explorer and a gray Chrysler Pacifica.

The moment Declan and Stella stepped from his vehicle, they watched as the door of the house opened and a tall and husky man in his mid to late forties came out, approaching them. He was wearing ranch clothes and a brown Stetson cowboy hat above short salt-and-pepper hair.

He regarded them with hard gray eyes and said in a steady voice, "I'm Jeb Stottlemire."

Declan said, "KBI special agent Delgado."

Stella identified herself, "FBI special agent Bailey."

Jeb shook their hands, and Declan asked him, "You reported that your daughter has been abducted?"

"Yeah. India, who just turned eight, was taken by her mother—and my ex-wife—Naomi Stottlemire," he responded tartly.

"Under what circumstances?" Stella asked him.

Jeb sucked in a deep breath and answered, "She showed up at India's elementary school on Boone Lane—before I could get there—and just took her. Because Naomi's her mother and lied about being given permission to pick India up, the school staff allowed it to happen."

"And you have full custody of your daughter?" Declan wanted to make it clear.

"Yeah, I do. Because of Naomi's history of drug abuse and suicidal behavior, the court recognized that India needed to be in a safe environment twenty-four seven." Jeb jutted his chin. "That would be in my custody. Now Naomi pulls a stunt like this!"

"Do you have any idea where she might have taken your daughter?" Stella asked him, glancing at the livestock grazing. "Perhaps back to wherever she lives?"

"Don't you think that was the first place I looked?" Jeb snapped. "Since our divorce last year, Naomi has been staying with her mother at a house on Olive Road in Bends Lake. According to her, Naomi never came home the night before—or since—and supposedly has not contacted the mother." He took off his hat and ran the back of his hand across a perspiring forehead. "I've tried to reach Naomi on her cell phone, but she won't pick up." His nostrils widened while eyeing Declan and Stella. "I'm worried about India. I fear what Naomi might try to do to her—"

So do I, Declan thought, meeting Stella's eyes, before he asked, "Has your ex-wife ever given you reason to believe that she might harm your daughter?"

"Not specifically," Jeb replied, putting his hat back on. "But she took India while unauthorized to do so. Even if I believe she loves our daughter in her own way, when Naomi does something as reckless and selfish as this, it makes me believe she's back to using drugs—antidepressants, cocaine and marijuana..."

"What type of car does Naomi drive?" Declan gazed at the missing girl's father, knowing that this was the easiest way to track her down through surveillance cameras.

Jeb replied, "A red Nissan Kicks."

As Declan took note, Stella said to Jeb, "We'll do everything we can to locate your daughter and ex-wife. Do you have recent photographs of them?"

"Yeah, I can pull them up from my cell phone," Jeb told her.

The images were sent to Stella's cell phone, and she, in turn, sent them to Declan's phone. He took one look at them and could see that Naomi Stottlemire was much younger than her husband. In her early thirties, she was blue-eyed and had straight blond hair in a blunt cut. India looked more like her mother than her father with long blond pigtails and big blue eyes. Physical similarities notwithstanding, Declan believed that the girl could be in danger.

By the time they left the property, he had put into motion the issuance of an Amber Alert, along with a request for the assistance of the KBI Child Victims Unit and Danver County Sheriff's Office's Exploited and Missing Child Unit. Stella had notified the FBI's local field office about the parental kidnapping and the Bureau's Child Abduction Rapid Deployment Team, in case they were needed, as she and Declan were well aware that the first few hours of a child's abduction were critical in locating the child unharmed and returning him or her home safe and sound.

Declan was on the road when he glanced at Stella and asked, "So, what's your read on Naomi Stottlemire and the likelihood that she would harm her daughter, for whatever reason? Especially if renewed substance abuse is part of the equation?"

After taking a moment or two to consider, Stella responded coolly. "Operating on limited info on the marital issues that resulted in a divorce and awarding Jeb full custody of India, my guess is that this is more an act of desperation by Naomi in wanting to be a greater part of her daughter's life—albeit an ill-advised move to be sure—and she probably has no wish to hurt her daughter." Stella took a breath, then said, "But even with the best of intentions, if Naomi was operating with drugs in her system, she may not be or may not have been thinking clearly in the decision to abduct her daughter from school. If this is the case, Naomi could still pose a real danger to India—one way or another—the longer they remain at large…"

"I'm thinking the same thing," Declan had to concur. "Which means we need to find the mother and daughter…and fast—"

Stella said, "Given the timeline, physical descriptions of the two and description of the car Naomi's likely to be driving, she couldn't have gotten far. Assuming that was her intention."

"Something tells me she didn't think this through, regardless of her state of mind when Naomi Stottlemire nabbed her daughter. Let's just hope for her sake—not to mention India's and Jeb's—that this can end peacefully."

"I'm with you there." Stella touched his pant leg. "We all want the same thing."

Declan had little doubt that they were on the same page. At least as law enforcement professionals. On the personal front, the jury was still out.

ABOUT AN HOUR LATER, the good news came. A sheriff's deputy spotted Naomi Stottlemire's Nissan Kicks with the help of a license plate reader on Lakmon Road in Bends Lake. The driver, identified by her license as the suspected parental abductor, was pulled over with her daughter, India, in the backseat and unharmed.

Naomi Stottlemire was placed under arrest, facing parental kidnapping charges, and the child was reunited with her father.

Stella, who was in the passenger seat of Declan's vehicle, breathed a sigh of relief. "Thank goodness India wasn't hurt in all this."

"I couldn't agree more." Declan briefly faced her while driving. "Let's just hope that her mother gets whatever help she needs and the girl doesn't have to suffer too much as her parents deal with their issues."

"Unfortunately, divorce and broken homes are part of life, whether we like it or not," Stella told him candidly. "Children are always the ones left to pay the price whenever parents decide to split up, though in some cases the dissolution of the marriage is actually in the child's or children's best interest."

"True." He drove closer to her hotel. "I doubt that would ever be the case when you get married—if children were ever in the picture."

She regarded his profile. "You think?"

"Don't you?" Declan bounced the question back at her. "From where I sit, it would always be in your children's best interest for the parents to stay together and work through any problems that come their way."

"Thanks." Stella felt her heart skip a beat in imagining such a scenario as marriage and family. "I could say the same for you. If you and Elise had been given a chance to have children, I'm sure they would have benefitted in each and every way."

"I agree." Declan paused. "It just wasn't meant to be with us," he reckoned. "Maybe I'll get a second crack at it."

"Maybe," she told him and mused, *Maybe I will experience such joy for the first time at some point.*

After he pulled up in front of the hotel, Declan eyed her and said flatly, "I don't suppose you'd like to invite me up for a drink?"

Stella turned to him and fluttered her lashes with interest. "Would you like to come up for a drink?" she asked daringly.

"Thought you'd never ask." He chuckled. "I'd love to."

She smiled with anticipation, even as Stella wondered just what she was getting herself into, while welcoming it nevertheless.

DECLAN STEPPED ONTO the balcony and gazed out at the lake. It was perfect at this time of year, but not nearly as perfect as he saw Stella in so many ways that he had not given proper attention to when they were together. Was it too late to acknowledge this?

He looked at her as she stood beside him, checking out the boaters. They were both holding cups of sparkling rosé wine. After taking a sip, Declan said, "I remember us taking a boat out there once." It belonged to a fellow KBI special agent, who had since retired.

"Me too." Stella smiled, tasting the wine. "It was fun."

"Yeah, it was." As were most things they did together back then. Declan found himself yearning for the good old days, even if they preceded his great relationship with Elise. But enjoying the company of Stella took nothing away from being with her sister. Or vice versa.

After they went back inside the room and put the emptied cups down, Declan studied Stella up close, liking everything he saw. He suddenly decided this was as good a time as any to do what he'd wanted to since practically the day they had laid eyes on one another again after three years. Or, at the very least, since they last kissed.

"Stella..." Declan touched her dainty chin. "You mind if I..." His words trailed off like a gust of wind, and as she made no attempt to stop him, he tilted his face ever so slightly and planted a nice kiss on her soft lips. Tasting the wine, he was more than happy to keep it going, and she seemed just as agreeable.

When Stella pulled away, touching her mouth, she eyed him ill at ease and asked tentatively, "What are we doing, Declan? Is this some sort of trip down memory lane for old times' sake? Or what?"

It was a good question, and he believed she deserved an answer that they both could live with. Holding her shoulders, Declan answered equably, "The memories of us together are great, by and large, Stella. But I don't see this as some sort of rekindling of yesteryear, per se. Instead, I prefer to view it as creating new memories and whatever they entail moving ahead..."

She held his gaze. "I like that."

With that, he cupped her cheeks, and they started kissing again. Though it felt perfectly natural to Declan to kiss Stella, and he found himself aroused and wanting to take this further—all the way to her bed—he resisted the impulse. If they were to pick up where they left off years ago, he wanted to do it right and safely, in both their best interests.

When the kiss ended, Declan sighed and said reluctantly, "I'd better go."

Stella nodded thoughtfully. "All right."

"See you when I see you," he told her at the door, and gave her one more quick kiss, then left before he could change his mind.

En route to his home, Declan felt good about the possibilities between him and Stella. Even if he understood realistically that there would be challenges that neither of them could run away from, even if they wanted to.

He pulled up alongside a basketball court and saw Aurelio Valderrama and a group of other young adults shooting hoops. When Aurelio spotted his car, he ran over to the passenger side, and Declan rolled down the window.

"Hey," Aurelio said, wearing a black sweat headband.

"What's up?" he asked him.

"We're short one guy." Aurelio rubbed his nose. "We could use another player. Are you game?"

Though Declan had more important things to do,

the competitive spirit in him couldn't resist the request. "Give me ten minutes to change."

"Cool." Aurelio flashed his teeth. "See you then."

He headed back to the court, and Declan drove off as his mind meandered between playing basketball, his current investigation and the sweet taste of Stella's lips when they kissed.

Chapter Eight

The next morning, Stella went jogging with fellow special agent Arielle Mendoza on a trail at Rendall Park on Velle Road. Both carried their official firearms as concealed weapons for personal protection in the event that they should be accosted by someone wishing them harm.

Strength in numbers, Stella told herself as they jogged through bur oak trees. Still on her mind was the kiss that, this time, Declan initiated. Not that she needed much convincing. She enjoyed the affection between them that seemed as natural as waking up to start a new day. What was yet to be determined was if these new memories he believed they were making had real legs. Or might they too wind up being untenable for the long run, as was the case the first time they tried to delve into something— only to fall flat?

"So, I'm thinking about applying for work in the Bureau's International Operations Division," Arielle said, with the sound of field sparrows chirping happily in the background.

Stella lifted a brow. "Really?"

"Yeah." Arielle wiped her brow with the back of her hand. "I'm currently unattached, fluent in Spanish and pretty well traveled. I'd love to work in South America or Europe in counterterrorism while taking in a different culture."

"Sounds great." Stella smiled at her. "If you feel strongly about this, I say go for it."

Arielle nodded. "Maybe I will." She sighed. "Do you plan to remain at the Detroit field office for a while?"

Stella stared at the question. A few days ago, she would have said definitely. Now she wasn't so sure after reconnecting with Declan. She would need time to consider other options that might materialize. She took a breath and told Arielle candidly, "I'm keeping an open mind on my future—wherever it leads me…"

Arielle grinned. "Nice way to look at things."

"I think so," Stella agreed. Just as she was contemplating this and the possibilities, they were stopped dead in their tracks when they came upon the body of an adult white male lying flat on his back in a pool of blood. She guessed him to be in his mid to late thirties and in good shape, with dark brown hair in a crew cut and a short, boxed beard. Wearing jogging clothes and black running shoes, he was lying just off the trail and, judging by the distinctive deep wounds to his chest, had been shot at least twice.

Instinctively, Stella and Arielle went for their firearms, not knowing if the shooter might still be lurking. They looked this way and that for any sign of danger, before deciding that the perp had apparently fled the scene and did not pose an immediate threat to their safety.

"Check him out," Arielle said, ill at ease nonetheless. "I'll cover you…"

"Okay." Stella put away her Glock 19 pistol long enough to crouch down and feel for a pulse. Albeit faint, she did detect one. "He's alive!" Her voice raised an octave with hope that the man could get through his victimization and come out okay on the other side. "Hang in there," she pleaded with him, though it was clear that the man was unconscious and hanging on for dear life.

"I'll call it in," Arielle said anxiously, tucking her gun back inside its holster and taking out her cell phone.

Stella nodded, her brow etched with worry as she regarded the man, knowing that both she and Arielle were thinking the same thing.

Apart from the fact that there appeared to be no gunshot injury to the head or face, the shooting bore all the trademarks of the Bends Lake Predator's modus operandi.

BEFORE HE ARRIVED at the crime scene, Declan had already begun calculating if the shooting that was reported by Stella and Arielle could actually have been the work of the unsub who had shot to death seven locals. Was this victim meant to be number eight? But had somehow managed to survive for now?

Guess I'll have to wait and see if the bullets pumped into the victim and spent shell casings that crime scene techs have already retrieved prove to be a match to the murder weapon used by the Bends Lake Predator, Declan told himself. He pulled into the parking lot with other law enforcement vehicles and an emergency medical services vehicle.

"You okay?" he asked Stella a couple of minutes later as Declan met up with her in the park. He noted that she was wearing jogging attire, which showed off her attractive, lean physique.

"I'm fine," she told him, her tone even as she faced the victim. "Wish I could say the same for him—identified by his driver's license as thirty-seven-year-old Blake Michaud III."

Declan regarded the man, who looked in pretty bad shape, as he was being placed on a gurney by paramedics. "Is he going to make it?"

"Don't know," Stella answered frankly. "He took two bullets to the chest, causing lots of damage." She sucked in a deep breath. "Based on their initial assessment, the EMTs seem to believe he has a fighting chance to survive—"

"That's the best we can hope for," Declan told her cautiously, and glanced around the wooded area. "Did you or Arielle—" whom he saw was conferring with police officers nearby "—see or hear anyone?"

"No." Stella shook her head. "Whoever shot him had apparently used a silencer and likely already had an escape route planned in advance."

"Hmm…" Declan made a face. "We'll have to see if any witnesses come forward. Or if surveillance cameras can help narrow down suspects."

Stella ran a hand across her forehead. "Even better would be if the victim can give us anything on his attacker to work with."

"Yeah, there is that," Declan agreed, as they both watched Blake Michaud III being carted off while fighting for his life.

THE BULLETS AND shell casings were a definite match with the ones fired from the Springfield Armory 1911 Ronin Operator 9 mm pistol that resulted in the deaths of seven people," Josephine Okamura told Declan on a video chat in his office a few hours later.

Leaning forward, he fixed the thirtysomething forensic analyst's narrow face on his laptop. It was surrounded by a brunette French-girl-chic hairstyle, and she was wearing geometric eyeglasses as Declan reaffirmed, "So, this attempted murder of Blake Michaud III was apparently a targeted shooting by the same unsub…?"

"No other way to look at it," she doubled down. "Same old, same old. Unless there's more than one shooter who used the same firearm."

"Not likely." Declan didn't believe for one minute, based on everything they knew, that there were two or more serial killers involved in the homicides. "The Bends Lake Predator has struck once again. Only this time, the unsub fell short—along with one bullet shy—of his customary outcome." *At least as of this moment, with the latest victim still clinging to life*, Declan thought.

Josephine touched her glasses and quipped, "The unsub must be losing his mojo. Or something else came up to break the pattern…"

"Yeah, maybe," Declan muttered, while wondering which applied. And if it was a troubling sign that could make the perp even more dangerous.

He was still somewhat perplexed on that front, though Declan had some thoughts on this as he wondered what Stella's take as a criminal profiler would be on what seemed to be a missed opportunity to get the job done by the unsub.

Declan briefed Kimberly Ullerich in her office on the latest development. She lowered her chin and said musingly, "Could be the break we've been looking for, assuming the victim survives and is able to reveal details on his would-be killer—"

"My sentiments exactly," Declan told her, thinking that a description of the unsub by a survivor could go a long way toward nabbing him. "I'll share this with the task force and see if we can begin to close in on the unsub."

Kimberly nodded. "Do that and let's find a way to bring him to justice before he goes after someone else…"

He left the field office for the Bends Lake Police Department for a task force update on the latest happenings in the investigation.

STELLA SAT BETWEEN Ursula and Arielle in the conference room as Declan started to brief them on the case. Or more specifically, the state of things with the most recent shooting victim and its relationship to the serial killer probe.

While holding the stylus pen at the front of the room, Declan regarded the touch screen display and said with a pained look on his face, "This morning, a thirty-seven-year-old, single businessman named Blake Michaud III was the victim of an attempted murder at Rendall Park." Declan put on the screen a recent photograph of the short-haired man, who was smiling and wearing a blue suit. "By chance, he was discovered seriously injured on a running trail by special agents Stella Bailey and Arielle Mendoza. Michaud had been shot twice in the chest. Ballistics confirmed that spent shell casings found at the scene and the bullets were a match and came from the same Springfield Armory 1911 Ronin Operator 9 mm pistol used to shoot to death seven other people. Such as the one you see on the screen."

Declan put up the image of a Ronin Operator 9 mm handgun as he said, "Paramedics rushed the victim to Bends Lake Hospital, where emergency surgery was performed. Though this was successful, according to staff, Michaud remains in critical condition, but it is believed that he will pull through. When we get the go-ahead, of course, we'll want to talk with the victim and see what he can tell us about the shooting—and most importantly, the shooter. In the meantime, an armed guard has been stationed outside Michaud's room, in the event that the perp tries to finish what he started."

After clearing the screen, Declan put up a montage of the dead victims, along with Blake Michaud III as the sole survivor of the Bends Lake Predator serial killer, and said with an edge to his voice, "This makes eight individuals who fell into the crosshairs of the unsub— with only one fortunate enough to have escaped death, as of now. Undoubtedly, this was made possible by the unsub mysteriously diverting from his usual MO by not shooting Michaud in the head..." Declan favored Stella with a direct look and said knowingly, "Perhaps Agent Bailey would like to address this?"

Yes, I would, Stella told herself, having expected this and given it some thought. She stood up and walked over to him, where she whispered in his ear, "I'll give it my best shot."

Declan smiled softly and gave her a friendly pat on the shoulder, then said in support, "Any thoughts you have would be appreciated."

She nodded and then eyed everyone else and waited

a beat before telling them in a clear voice, "When I first came upon the victim while running at Rendall Park, noting the similarities of the shooting to victims who were shot dead by the serial killer, my first thoughts were that the unsub may have been spooked by my presence, along with Arielle's, and was forced to flee the scene prematurely, at the risk of being exposed and having to deal with that."

Stella sucked in a calming breath and continued, "I still think that's a good possibility in explaining why the unsub didn't shoot the latest victim in the face or head. But there's also good reason to believe that the serial killer's gun could've jammed. Or run out of ammo, as a mistake on his part in not checking ahead of time." She kept her shoulders even. "Bottom line, from my perspective, is that it was the unsub's full intention to murder the victim in the manner the killer was accustomed to—but his plans were thwarted through one means or another—saving the life of Blake Michaud III. And possibly endangering others, as the unsub may attempt to make up for this mistake by finding a replacement victim, sooner than later—"

"WOULD YOU LIKE to have dinner with me at my place tonight?" Declan pulled Stella to the side as the task force members dispersed after the briefing. With the latest victim still sedated and not expected to be in a position to be interviewed till morning, now seemed an opportune moment for Declan to see if she was ready and willing to move past her hesitancy in revisiting the house he lived in with Elise—but was now void of the energy she brought to it. He believed Stella could do the same, and more, if she only gave it—them—a real chance.

"Yes, I'm up for that." She met his eyes steadfastly. "I think Elise would probably feel that it's high time."

Declan grinned. "I agree." He felt relieved that she was on board. Where they went from there would be up to them. "How does seven sound?"

"Perfect." She smiled. "Shall I bring anything?"

"Just yourself will do," he answered smoothly. It was more than enough to make for a pleasant meal.

Stella nodded. "All right."

Declan watched her walk away, and he spoke for a few minutes with some members of the task force who were still in the room, before heading out himself. He was admittedly excited about being able to cook for Stella, as not only a respite from their official duties, but another step toward one another.

After dropping by a supermarket on the way home to pick up some items for dinner that he believed would appeal to Stella's tastebuds, Declan was back in his car and on the road. While his thoughts meandered between the investigation and Stella being back in his life, he could only wonder if there was some symmetry there that could only lead to good things, when the dust settled.

STELLA WAS TRULY a bundle of nerves as she drove toward Declan's house for the first time since returning to Bends Lake, having avoided it like the plague for probably all the wrong reasons. *It's time that I put the demons to rest*, she told herself while studying the road. Elise was gone and so was her marriage to Declan. *But I'm still here and so is he. We both deserve just as much happiness in life, should it come our way,* Stella mused as the familiar landscape came into view. Even if that happiness could be short-lived, with geography still an issue. At least as things stood at the moment.

Stella thought briefly about coming upon the victim of an attempted murder during her run—at the hands of the unsub known as the Bends Lake Predator. Being with the Bureau, she'd encountered violence before. But it was usually in the line of duty. She had been shaken somewhat in becoming a witness after the fact to a man shot twice and left for dead. The fact that it appeared he would survive the ordeal, and possibly be able to help them apprehend his attacker, gave her solace, even if Stella knew this could only be complete when the investigation had run its course.

She pulled up next to Declan's vehicle, while marveling at the property he owned and the wetland, having practically forgotten what a great piece of land it was—including the farmhouse itself.

Stella ran a hand through her long hair, which was loose. She took one look at her attire—a mocha puffed-sleeve midi dress and slingback sandals—and decided it was satisfying enough for the date. Was that what this was? Or was it simply a meal between two acquaintances who had to eat?

Before she reached the front door of the house, it opened and Declan filled the door nicely. Freshly shaven and his hair still wet from showering, he was wearing a light blue linen button-up shirt, beige slacks and brown loafers.

She met his eyes. "Hey."

"Hey." He grinned at her. "Glad you remembered how to get here," he joked.

Her eyes batted playfully. "Guess there are some things you never forget."

"Guess you're right." Declan flashed a thoughtful look. "Come in."

The moment she stepped inside the house, Stella felt the memories come flooding back as though from only yesterday, while she took it all in—knowing that Elise had left her mark on the decor and loving her sister for that.

"Make yourself at home," Declan cut into her thoughts, "and I mean that sincerely."

"I will." She smiled as her nostrils picked up the scent of food. "Smells good."

"Should taste even better," he bragged. "I made grilled halibut with tomato vinaigrette, sliced red potatoes and herbed ricotta biscuits—serving it with white wine."

"That does sound delicious," she had to admit, having forgotten just what a good cook he was when they dated.

He seemed to read her mind as he said, "Being on my own, I don't really invest much time in cooking very much these days—but I can still bring it when duty calls."

"Never doubted it." She chuckled. "So, what can I do to help?"

"You can relax." He angled his face. "Or if you really want to help, you can open the wine and fill the wineglasses."

"I'll go with the latter option." She grinned, feeling that this was the least she could do to be a small part of the process.

"So be it," he agreed. "I'm sure you remember where the glasses are kept?"

Stella laughed. "I think I can find them."

They sat on retro faux-leather chairs in the dining room across a mid-century modern solid wood table from each other.

"My compliments to the chef," Stella had to say honestly, after sinking her teeth into the mouthwatering grilled halibut.

"Thanks." Declan grinned sheepishly. "Good to know that I haven't lost my touch."

"Not even a little," she assured him, and stuck a fork into a red potato.

"Well, there's more where that came from," he told her in a teasing manner before sipping wine.

"I'll bet." Stella wondered if there was a double meaning there, as a wave of desire swept over her like a sudden rise in body temperature. Was he feeling this too? If so, what should they do about it?

By the time the meal was over, that speculation was put to rest. They brought their goblets of wine into the great room, finished them off and started to kiss like crazy.

Feeling light in her head and on her feet, Stella uttered between his lips brazenly, "I want you, Declan."

He unlocked their mouths and, while peering into her eyes, responded intently, "Are you sure about that?"

She hesitated for a moment, meeting his hard gaze. "Yes," she uttered unwaveringly.

Declan lifted her chin and said fervently, "Then I may as well be honest when I tell you, Stella, that I want you more, if that's possible."

"Not sure it is possible..." she confessed blushingly, laying her cards on the table. They had been building up to this moment, slowly but surely, since the time she returned to Bends Lake. And there was no denying it. "At the very least, I'd say that we're on pretty much equal footing here," Stella offered, meeting him halfway.

Declan grinned excitedly. "I can live with that."

Her teeth shone. "So can I."

"Then let's live...together—"

They moved back toward one another and kissed more passionately, causing Stella's body to tingle wildly all over, before she forced herself to ask him in a responsible way, "Do you have any protection?" If they were ever to procreate, she wanted it to be planned and with mutual consent in bringing precious children into the world.

"Yes," he assured her and took Stella's hand. "Come with me..."

They mounted the stairs to the second floor, where Declan led her to the primary suite, a large room with traditional furniture and a king sleigh bed that had a patchwork quilt on it. He opened a drawer in a rattan nightstand and removed a pack containing a latex condom. It was all Stella needed to see to up her desire to be with him a notch—maybe a few notches—as they began to quickly undress and allow nature to take its course.

Chapter Nine

Stella was all in as she traced every square inch of Declan's rock-hard body in the nude, bringing about an awareness of familiarity. She felt a tad self-conscious as his eyes studied her nakedness from head to toe, till turning his gaze to meet her own, and Stella could see the raw desire in them. It put her at ease and, at the same time, solidified her own wish to be with him.

It feels so right, Stella told herself as, while still standing, they moved up to one another and started to kiss in an all-consuming way that was giving them all the buildup needed to take things to the next level.

When Declan pulled away from her, he gave Stella a once-over again and declared, "You're so beautiful—all of you!"

"Umm..." was all she could think to say in a blushing response, before Stella told him candidly, "That makes two of us."

"If you say so," he said huskily. "We both deserve this as beautiful people hot for each other!"

"Show me," she uttered, barely able to hold her composure in wanting to be with him.

Without ado, Stella found herself being swept into Declan's powerful arms and carried to the bed. He laid her down on the sateen sheet, put on the protection and slid beside her.

As Stella reached for him, eager to feel his weight upon her and the sexual relations in motion, Declan said smoothly, "Not just yet. I want you to lay back and enjoy this…"

She watched with interest as he used his deft fingers and firm mouth to stimulate her from head to feet and toes, bringing Stella to the brink. She read the hunger for her in his eyes, matching hers for him. When she could stand it no more, she voiced lustfully, "Declan, make love to me—right now!"

He got the message, loud and clear, responding, "If you insist."

"Yes, I do," she uttered vivaciously.

"Then say no more!"

On that note, Declan smoothly positioned himself between her splayed legs, and Stella winced with pleasure as he gave her a hearty kiss and drove deep inside her. She dug her nails into his broad shoulders, and they clung together as the heat rose a few notches at the start of their lovemaking.

Almost instantly, Stella felt her climax roar through her body like a wildfire and she cried out, quivering with the tremendous impact.

Only when she had calmed down did Declan plunge further into her, their bodies slick with perspiration, and shortly thereafter had his own potent release. Simultaneously, a second orgasm ensued for Stella, as they rode the rapids of intimacy till thoroughly satiated.

Afterward, while side by side and catching their breaths, Declan chuckled and said, "Wow! That was amazing!"

She laughed. "You think so, do you?"

"Don't you?" He looked at her.

Stella blushed. "How could I not?"

Declan rested a hand on her knee. "Some things in life are worth the wait."

"I agree," she told him as a case of déjà vu flashed in her head. Then she added, without giving it much thought, "Other things can't happen soon enough." *Did I just say that?* Stella asked herself as she met his eyes. Since when had she become so forward where it concerned such intimate and sincere thoughts?

"Right on that score too," he concurred. "What's meant to be is meant to be—no matter the obstacles that may get in the way."

Stella chewed on his philosophical words, wondering if they were truly meant to be, as if they'd been waiting their turn. Or was what just happened more indicative of pent-up needs than a gateway to the future and coming attractions?

AFTER A BRIEF PAUSE, they went at it a second round. Only this time, Declan was able to take his own sweet time in exploring Stella's perfect body—from her gorgeous face to firm, medium-size breasts to shapely legs and feet—and intoxicating scent, without the encumbrance of needing to keep his libido in check till she had been satisfied.

Instead, they got to bridge the gap between being totally aroused with each other and fulfilling that need by reaching a peak of pleasure—like climbing Kansas's Mount Sunflower—before tumbling back down to earth, left still wanting more.

That came during the wee hours of the morning—with

more satisfaction both ways—after which Declan held Stella as if never wanting to let go, as she fell asleep. The truth was, she had proven to be much more than he could have asked for in rediscovering each other.

But he wanted to ask for more of her. A lot more. Problem was, he didn't quite know how to do this. Not without the risk of losing her again. *Do I really want to put either of us through that a second time?* Declan asked himself, knowing there wouldn't be an Elise to come into his life the way she had, should he fail. Nor would he want to pursue anyone else, with Stella such a good fit. A very good one, in fact.

But did she feel the same way beyond their feverish night together?

Declan allowed this to weigh on his mind before drifting off to sleep. He awakened in the morning and watched Stella as she slept peacefully. He wanted to see this vision time and time again, if it were possible—with them sharing the same bed. Again, he wondered if this was asking for too much.

When she opened her eyes and stared at him, Stella said, smiling, "How long have you been awake?"

"Long enough to enjoy watching you in your beauty sleep," he said coolly.

She chuckled. "Hope I wasn't snoring?"

"You weren't." Declan regarded her thoughtfully. "Why don't you stay here for the rest of your time in Bends Lake?" he suggested.

Stella met his gaze. After a moment or two, she asked tentatively, "Is that what you really want?"

"Yeah, definitely." Declan made no bones about it, but he still didn't want to put any undue pressure on her or scare her off. "Look, you can use a guest room, if you like, and have the run of the place, which is a lot more comfortable than a hotel—even though you do have a nice view from the deck." He paused. "Say yes," he prodded gently.

"Okay, yes," Stella acquiesced. "You win, I'll move out of the hotel."

Declan grinned. "Good." He glanced at her outline beneath the sheet, imagining her beauty in the nude. Just then, his cell phone rang. He stretched his long arm and grabbed it off the nightstand and saw that the caller was Ursula.

"Better get that," he told Stella, who nodded, as he said over the phone, "Hey."

Ursula got straight to the point when she said, "Blake Michaud is awake and apparently able to talk."

Declan reacted positively to the news. "That's great."

"I'm heading to the hospital right now."

"I'll meet you there," he told her and disconnected, then relayed the information to Stella.

"I'll go with you," she said, and started to get up.

"Not necessary," he told her succinctly. "The victim may not have much to offer. Stay here and rest up a bit more—after not getting much sleep last night."

She batted her eyes. "And whose fault was that?" she teased him.

"Guilty as charged." He colored as intimate thoughts crossed his mind, and he was perfectly okay with taking responsibility for their blazing sexual activity—even if she had proven to be more than able to hold her own.

Stella laughed with a yawn. "Me too."

"I'll accept that." Declan climbed out of bed. "I'm

going to go take a quick shower. I'll leave the spare key on the island in the kitchen." He leaned over and gave her a sweet kiss. "Catch you later."

STELLA WATCHED DECLAN'S firm backside as he stepped inside the en suite bathroom. She had a mind to join him, but thought better of it as he had a job to do without being distracted or otherwise slowed down by her while in pursuit of a wicked serial killer.

Leaning her head back against the fluffy pillow, Stella closed her eyes for what was supposed to be a moment, after getting little sleep. Only when she opened them, she realized that just enough time had passed that Declan had showered, dressed and left her a little note to say how much he enjoyed her company and hoped to have more of it.

I feel the same way, she told herself, stretching her legs and flexing her toes.

Stella's thoughts turned to the night of unbridled passion with Declan. It tapped into every nerve in her body and reminded her of what she'd been missing in her life since their relationship ended. But there was no second-guessing. She believed that most things happened for a reason, and that was probably true for how things fell apart for them previously.

As for this time around, she was keeping her options open as to what she should read into it. Hot sex was not enough in and of itself to consider uprooting her life. Or Declan's, for that matter. But the chemistry between them could not be denied. Nor her sense of belonging as she lay in his bed, still picking up his invigorating manly scent.

Being invited to spend the remainder of her stay in

town at the house made perfect sense to Stella. As a practical matter, it would make it easier for them to spend time together when operating under one roof—no matter how much time they had to work with. And should things progress between them to a whole new level, they could take it from there and see where it went—if, in fact, they were meant to go somewhere special.

She forced herself to roll out of bed, shower and get dressed before Stella poured herself a cup of coffee that Declan had made fresh. After drinking it, she headed back to the hotel to pack her bags for a return trip to the house that was beginning to feel a lot like home. Only she had a home in Detroit—and parents who also had begun a life there.

Was upending that a wise move? Or even possible, career-wise?

Don't get ahead of yourself, Stella told herself as she parked in the lot and went inside the hotel, determined not to blow a good thing with Declan. Assuming he felt the same way about her, and they could both agree on exactly what they wanted—or even expected—from each other.

AFTER A STOP at the field office, Declan headed toward Bends Lake Hospital, bringing back memories of Elise working there in the field of occupational therapy. She was great at what she did, and he was proud of her for following through on a dream. Just as he had in pursuing a career in law enforcement.

Now he was pursuing Elise's sister, whom Declan had met first and never was able to quite get out of his mind with the connection they had. Maybe it was all meant to come full circle, even if they had to get through some detours in the process of life.

Only time would tell.

For now, he was more than willing to play the hand both had been dealt and see how far they could get in the final analysis.

Declan reached the hospital and met up with Ursula inside the ICU waiting room. He asked her, "Have you spoken to Michaud?"

"Not yet," she replied. "The doctor's with him now."

I hope he can shed some light on the unsub that will lead to identifying him, Declan mused. "Has any surveillance video surfaced on a possible suspect?"

"We're still working on that." Ursula relaxed her shoulders. "Maybe whatever Michaud can tell us will provide some clarity that can correspond with any security camera footage that comes into play."

Declan nodded in agreement. Both turned as they were approached by a fortysomething, slender male with red hair in a short fade cut and a Balbo beard. He was wearing doctors' scrubs.

"I'm Dr. Hunt," he said.

"Special Agent Delgado," Declan told him.

Ursula followed with "Special Agent Liebert."

Hunt nodded at them. "You can go in to speak with Mr. Michaud now—but only for a few minutes. Though he managed to survive two bullets shot at close range, he still sustained some damage and is very weak, a bit disoriented and faces a long period of recovery."

"Got it," Declan told him, while eager to speak to the victim.

They went inside the room and saw what was expected

with the typical machines, tubes and wires. Blake Michaud III was lying on the bed looking miserable, though no doubt he was glad to be alive after his ordeal.

After they identified themselves and flashed their IDs, with both standing on one side of the bed, Declan said straightforwardly, "Can you tell us what you remember about your attack?"

Blake winced and said in a strained voice, "I was jogging in the park, minding my own business—when this guy came out from the trees, blocking my path..."

"And then?" Ursula prodded him.

He drew a breath and continued, "The man had a gun in his hand. He pointed it at me and said coldly, 'You're going to die.' I said, 'What?'" Blake's brow furrowed. "He replied, 'I'm the Bends Lake Predator. See you in hell—maybe...' That's when he shot me..."

Declan was glad that the unsub confirmed what had already been established—if only for the record. But it still didn't explain why only two shots instead of three, per the unsub's MO.

Just as Ursula started to ask the victim about this, Blake licked dry lips and said, "I remember that he pointed the gun at my face and pulled the trigger. But the gun was empty. I wasn't sure if he would reload or what—but passed out at that point, not knowing if I would ever wake up again..."

"You got lucky," Declan told him bluntly, sure that he had already made that calculus—even if he probably wasn't feeling it at the moment, while recovering from his injuries.

Blake muttered, "Yeah, I suppose."

Ursula leaned toward him and said, a catch to her

voice, "I have to ask, do you have any enemies—or know of anyone who might want to do you harm…take your life—?"

Blake considered the question for a long moment then responded surely, "I don't know anyone in my business or personal life who wants to kill me." He sighed. "Believe me, if I did, I would tell you."

Declan had no reason to doubt him. Even if his pursuit of success in the retail sector could be cutthroat, his rivals shouldn't resort to murder—unless there was more to the man than met the eye, including unrelated to work. "Can you describe the man who attacked you?"

Blake twisted his lips thoughtfully before replying, "Honestly, I didn't get a good look at him—it all happened so fast—and my mind's a bit fuzzy…but I can try," he said.

After they got the description, Declan asked Blake if he would be up for talking to a forensic sketch artist, and he agreed. They got the doctor's permission and set things in motion for what Declan hoped might result in pinpointing the unsub's identity.

STELLA CHECKED OUT of her room, put her bags in the car and went back inside the hotel to say goodbye to Gayle Reese, having spotted her earlier at work.

Stepping inside the gift shop, Stella saw Gayle chatting amicably with a tall and fit thirtysomething male. He had black hair, styled in a number three buzz cut, a high forehead and a designer stubble beard. Dressed in casual clothing and oxfords, he stopped talking in following the flight of Gayle's gaze and regarded Stella curiously with eyes that were solid blue.

"Hey," Gayle said to her, smiling.

"Hey." Stella smiled back.

"This is my cousin, Lochlyn." Gayle angled her face at him and back. "This is Stella. We went to high school together. Ran into each other here at the hotel, where she's staying."

Stella met his eyes. "Hi."

"Hello." He grinned. "That was obviously after I had graduated from Bends Lake High, having attended a few years before Gayle started. Sorry we missed each other."

Stella took that as harmless flirtation and said, "We all have our time period in school and can only make the most of it."

"Very true," he said evenly and studied her. "So, where do you live these days?"

"Detroit." Stella assumed he was still local, so didn't bother to ask otherwise.

"Cool." Lochlyn smiled and regarded Gayle. "Well, I'll leave you two to talk. Are we still on for tennis this afternoon?"

"Yes," Gayle told him. "I'll be at the court as scheduled."

"Okay. See you then." He looked at Stella. "Nice to meet you."

"You too," she said.

Lochlyn headed off and took a cell phone out of his chinos, tapped it and put it up to his ear as he left the gift shop.

"Cousin, huh?" Stella said as she faced Gayle while they stood by a display of souvenirs.

"Yeah. Lochlyn's really been more like a big brother to me over the years, not having a biological one," Gayle remarked. "He helped me deal with going through the divorce, having been there himself."

"Glad he was there for you." Stella was thankful that she'd never had to go down that road as she wanted a marriage that would last a lifetime, if possible. "Anyway, just wanted to let you know I've checked out of the hotel."

"Oh?" Gayle's eyes widened. "Sorry you're leaving."

I'm not actually, Stella thought, but didn't feel they were quite close enough right now to dish out the details of her love life and its potential. "Me too," she told her sincerely. "Let's keep in touch."

Gayle nodded. "Absolutely."

They exchanged phone numbers, and Stella left as Gayle went to help a customer.

When she got back to Declan's farmhouse, Stella resolved to get past any weird feelings of being in a place her sister once occupied as woman of the house. She missed Elise dearly but needed to live in the present, with an eye toward the future. Which may or may not include Declan.

Settling into one of the guestrooms, which was bright and cheery with its own en suite bathroom, Stella felt more comfortable, at this point, having her own space while there. Even if she wound up in Declan's bed at night, if the passion they shared was sustainable.

She unpacked her things then took out her cell phone and called her mother for a quick catch up, nonchalantly mentioning that her stay in Bends Lake had been extended, without elaborating further.

Chapter Ten

That afternoon, the search was on for a serial killer suspect named Joaquin Kalember. The thirty-nine-year-old ex-con became a person of interest in the case after shooting victim Blake Michaud III described his attacker to forensic sketch artist Helene Davidovich.

Using sketch recognition software, Declan and the team were able to match the forensic sketch to a close enough degree to Kalember's mug shot. A known sex offender with a history of violence and predilection for child pornography, Kalember had been fingered by Michaud. His body type also conformed to the description provided by the victim. Furthermore, Kalember was caught on surveillance video near the park where the crime occurred, giving Declan even more reason to think he could be the person they sought. Declan wanted to bring in the suspect for questioning.

When Bends Lake police officers spotted Joaquin Kalember driving a dark blue Kia Sportage SUV that was registered to his name on Heptor Street, the car was pulled over and the unarmed suspect taken into custody without resisting arrest.

Now that Kalember was off the streets, before he was interrogated, Declan wanted to have all his ducks in a row. He secured a search warrant for the suspect's residence and cell phone, hoping to find direct evidence that linked Kalember to the shootings.

Wearing ballistic body armor, Declan and Ursula, bolstered by personnel from the KBI's Special Operations Division, the Danver County Sheriff's Office's Criminal Investigations Division and a K-9 unit from the Bends Lake Police Department, converged upon the Wylson Mobile Home Park on Pletcher Road, where they executed the warrant.

With no one present, the order was given by Declan to break the door down to the manufactured home. They stormed inside the cramped place with two bedrooms and well-worn furnishings, and a search ensued for a Springfield Armory 1911 Ronin Operator 9 mm handgun and ammunition. Along with any other relevant indicators of the suspect's complicity in the serial murders that had terrorized the residents of Bends Lake for more than six months.

"Find anything?" Declan eyed the team at work.

"Nothing that ties Kalember as yet to the Bends Lake Predator's crimes," Ursula answered, a sound of disappointment in her tone.

"Keep at it," he directed her and the others on hand, while moving about himself, wearing nitrile gloves.

By the time the search was completed, inside and out, no murder weapon was found. Or ammo.

The suspect, though, was found to be in possession of child sexual abuse material and illegal narcotics, including cocaine and fentanyl pills.

While Kalember would have to answer for these serious offenses, Declan's current objective was to get the suspect in front of him as it pertained to the serial killer case.

Half an hour later, he was sitting across the table from Joaquin Kalember in an interrogation room. Declan took a moment to size up the suspect, who looked fairly similar to the composite sketch rendered by the forensic artist. Of course, she was only as good as the description given of the shooter. Though the suspect's mug shot was spot on, Declan could still detect slight differences, as Kalember's face was a bit narrower, nose a little longer and chin not quite as protruding. The suspect's close-set blue eyes were bloodshot, and his short dark hair was in a modern mullet.

Declan gazed sharply at him and said, "You're in serious trouble, with the child porn found at your house and on your cell phone, as well as the drugs confiscated from your residence—but right now, I want to talk about an attempted murder in which you've been implicated…"

"What?" Declan watched the color drain from the suspect's face as Kalember argued, "I don't know what the hell you're talking about…"

Leaning forward, Declan drew his brows together and said flatly, "The victim described to a sketch artist the man who shot him yesterday morning at Rendall Park. This matched your mug shot. Surveillance video spotted you leaving the area around the same time. I have to say, this doesn't look good for you, Kalember," he told him in no uncertain terms.

Kalember, who was not cuffed—but in no position to take Declan on, if it came down to Declan needing to defend himself from the suspect—ran a hand across his mouth then responded ill at ease, "I met a woman at the park to sell drugs to, then we went our separate ways—that's it! If someone described me to a sketch artist, he was wrong. I didn't shoot anyone—"

Declan peered at him dubiously. "I need the name of this person you say you sold drugs to—and where I can find her to verify your story." As the suspect pondered ratting out the drug user, Declan added, "Believe me, it's in your best interest—and hers—to cooperate. Otherwise, you could be facing an attempted murder rap..." *And that's only the start of the homicide-related charges that could be coming your way*, Declan thought.

Kalember seemed to get the picture and spilled the beans regarding his drug transaction. For Declan, even if he would have loved to coax a confession out of Kalember, given the lack of an attempted murder weapon—to say nothing of being unable to link the suspect to the seven actual murders committed with the same Ronin Operator 9 mm pistol—the evidence simply wasn't there to support the contention that Kalember was the Bends Lake Predator.

Declan was left with no real choice but to accept this for what it was. As Blake Michaud was admittedly fuzzy about his recollections, he was apparently off in his description of his attacker. Or, if accurate, it was someone who looked like Joaquin Kalember, but he wasn't the one who tried to kill Michaud.

Meaning that the true killer was still on the loose—and as dangerous as ever—while the hunt for him had been temporarily sidetracked.

Though Kalember's alibi had yet to be confirmed, as far as Declan was concerned, his troubles—which could have him put away for a long time—did not include a failed attempt to gun down Blake Michaud in a manner that had already been successful with seven others.

AT THE WYLSON MOBILE HOME PARK, the Bends Lake Predator watched through the window of his manufactured home as law enforcement was still coming in and out of Joaquin Kalember's place. Why had they hauled him in? Had one of the neighbors tipped off the authorities that Joaquin was dealing drugs?

Or worse, rumor had it that he was into child porn.

Whichever way he sliced it, the Bends Lake Predator had no sympathy whatsoever for anyone who crossed the line the way Joaquin was thought to have. He fully deserved whatever he had coming to him.

By comparison, his own misdeeds were much more acceptable to the serial killer. In his way of thinking, those who took bullets from his hand needed to die. He had the ultimate power over their lives and deaths—and chose to pull the rug from beneath them by taking away anything and everything they stood for in practically the blink of an eye.

Knowing that their fate was sealed—just as sure as being diagnosed with a terminal illness—he watched the light go out of their eyes as the reality of losing any control over their own destiny set in morbidly.

Except for the execution that went awry. It had been his every intention to end a life at Rendall Park. Instead, his firearm failed him at the very moment of eliminating the target. Without having the ammo to finish the job and with footsteps approaching, he was left with no choice but to leave his prey and hope the two bullets pumped into the man's chest would still get the job done.

But this failed.

The runner survived and was apparently on his way to making a full recovery.

Damn him.

The Bends Lake Predator cursed his rotten luck in this instance. He knew it would be all but impossible to finish the job.

And so he would have to make up for it with someone else, for he would not be denied. Two for the price of one.

He continued to gaze out the window at the activity underway and couldn't help but crack a grin at the thought that the authorities had the Bends Lake Predator right under their collective noses and, sadly, weren't the wiser.

Their terrible misfortune would be his gain once more.

STELLA DID NOT necessarily consider cooking to be her strongest suit, but she'd learned just enough from her mother and Elise to be able to create a decent meal if she put her mind to it. Being used to takeout, quick meals and restaurant dining during her busy life as an FBI behavioral analyst, she decided to step up her game by making dinner as Declan's houseguest. After making a stop at the supermarket, she had gathered the ingredients she needed to make a corn pudding casserole, barbecue chicken breasts baked in the oven, fried green tomatoes and zucchini bread. It was the least she could do in carrying her own weight—even if she was uncertain just how long her stay would be here, with neither of them looking much beyond the moment at hand.

While preparing everything in the kitchen, Stella's thoughts wandered to the news she'd received from

Declan that the sketch of the attacker as described by Michaud had not panned out. The mug shot of suspect Joaquin Kalember, which resembled the facial composite, turned out to be misleading, as Kalember's alibi checked out.

Meaning that Blake Michaud's assailant was still out there.

This disturbed Stella as she, like everyone else, just wanted this to be over with by nailing the serial killer. But it would be longer now before he could be apprehended for his crimes.

At least in going after Joaquin Kalember, they were able to serendipitously uncover his penchant for child pornography and dealing in illegal drugs—both of which were intolerable—taking him off the streets for their trouble.

Stella's mind turned back to the task at hand, as she put the finishing touches on the meal and grabbed the bottle of white wine from the fridge they had opened the day before.

By the time Declan had arrived home, having given her a heads-up, she had already set the table and was ready to eat.

"Hey!" Stella told him coolly when he walked through the door. She hoped that a good meal might take his mind off the disappointment of not being able to put the brakes on his investigation with an arrest.

"What's this?" Declan looked genuinely surprised. "You cooked dinner?"

"Yes." She laughed. "I wanted to return the favor."

He lifted a brow whimsically. "Okay."

She told him, for context, "I seem to recall cooking for you once or twice back in the day."

"Yeah, I remember." He chuckled. "Glad to see that you were comfortable enough here to go for it."

Stella blushed. "I'm getting there," she confessed, maybe more than she cared to admit. "Why don't you wash up, and I'll put the food out, and you can tell me just how tasty it is."

"Sounds like a plan," he said, grinning at her in a way that reminded Stella of just how good-looking Declan was, along with how sexy. Both had served him well and made it relatively easy to fall for him again.

Fifteen minutes later, they were sitting at the dining room table eating. Stella watched tensely as Declan dug into the corn pudding casserole and said, "Looks like I'll have some competition in the kitchen. This is amazing!"

"Glad you like it." Her teeth shone. "Runs in the family," she told him, paying homage to Elise and her parents.

"I can see that." He smiled at Stella then lifted a slice of zucchini bread and bit into it. "Bloodline has its place, but your abilities in and out of the kitchen succeed on their own merits."

"Nice of you to think so," she said, not about to argue the point.

"I know so," he doubled down, and sipped wine.

Stella told him candidly, "Your merits are just as rock solid."

"I suppose." Declan nodded. "Must be why we get along so well."

"Among other reasons," she said coquettishly.

"True," he concurred musingly while forking a tomato.

Stella sank her teeth into a piece of chicken, and they talked about the latest twist in the serial killer investigation.

"I thought we might have had him dead to rights," Declan griped. "But it was not to be."

"These things happen," she said in defense of Blake Michaud and his faulty depiction of the unsub who tried to kill him. "We both know that trying to describe an attacker after being under duress at the time of the attack is wholly unreliable—especially after the disorienting trauma of being shot twice in the process."

"Spoken like a true profiler," Declan said with a laugh. "I take your point, though. Michaud was off on his description, and that's the way it goes. The fact that he survived at all, and that the unsub fell short of his intentions, was a major victory in and of itself."

"I agree." Stella dabbed a napkin to her mouth. Though she wondered what this meant in the long run with an unhinged serial killer still out there and possibly looking for retribution after failing to complete another kill, she had to say, "At least the composite sketch resulted in nabbing someone who was into child porn and drug dealing."

Declan responded in concurrence, "That was definitely a good thing."

"I think so," she said, taking each victory as it came in the often unpredictable world of law enforcement.

They went to bed, where Stella took the bold initiative of exploring Declan up and down, wanting to reacquaint herself with him in every way—and enjoying everything he had to offer, which was plenty.

In turn, he gave her just as much pleasure, and more,

while they made love for hours—till sheer exhaustion and full sexual satisfaction overcame them, and they fell asleep in each other's arms.

But before she drifted off, Stella felt that she was falling in love with Declan all over again, as if that raw emotion had been hidden even from herself over the years and was now coming back with a sweet vengeance. Even if she wasn't quite sure how to process it. Or how he would.

DECLAN HAD BEEN enjoying an erotic dream, where he and Stella picked up where they left off in the real world in his bedroom, when he was jarred awake by a ringing sound. Opening his eyes, he still heard it and quickly realized that it was his doorbell ringing. He grabbed his cell phone from the nightstand and saw that it was 10:00 p.m. There was also a text message from Aurelio Valderrama that read succinctly:

Need to see you. On my way over. Important.

As Declan assessed this, the doorbell rang again. He saw Stella rousing awake. "Is that your bell?" she asked in a sleepy voice.

"Yeah. Got a text from a local kid I play basketball with. He's at the door." Declan sighed musingly. "I need to see what this is all about."

Stella lifted on an elbow. "Do you want me to come with you?"

"Not necessary," he answered, knowing that she was naked beneath the cover and sheet and seeing no reason for her to put on clothes just yet. "I won't be long."

Declan kissed Stella on the mouth and rolled out of

bed. He grabbed a pair of jeans and a T-shirt off a gray accent chair in the corner of the room and quickly donned them before heading downstairs in his bare feet.

While contemplating what could be so urgent that Aurelio needed to show up at his door, Declan considered that he and his younger sister lived with a single mother—with the father having long been out of the picture. As far as Declan knew, the kid hadn't gotten into trouble beyond the normal teenage issues of drinking and vandalism—neither of which had landed him in the juvenile justice system. But the pressures were always there among peers to delve into other behaviors that could land him in hot water. Was that the case here?

When he opened the door, Declan stared at Aurelio, who looked nervous and was wearing his typical basketball attire. He was holding a brown paper bag.

"Hey—sorry to just show up like this," Aurelio stammered. "But thought it was best to talk in person."

"This better be good," Declan said stiffly, though intrigued nonetheless. "Come in."

Once inside, Aurelio gazed down at his sneakers and looked up at Declan tentatively and said, "I have something you need to see..."

He handed him the bag, and Declan said curiously, "What is it?"

Aurelio took a breath. "Just take a look."

"Okay." Declan opened the bag and saw that there was a handgun inside. He glanced at Aurelio and back at the weapon, studying it as he asked the kid uneasily, "What are you doing with this?"

Before Aurelio could respond, Declan's heart skipped a beat as he recognized the firearm as a Springfield Armory 1911 Ronin Operator 9 mm pistol with a suppressor. Just like the weapon used by the Bends Lake Predator serial killer to shoot eight people—seven fatally.

Chapter Eleven

After Stella got dressed and joined them, as Declan had a feeling this was something she needed to hear, he introduced her as Special Agent Bailey—figuring that Aurelio was wise enough to draw the correct conclusions that they were romantically involved. Besides that, Declan knew that discovering he had company at night was the least of the kid's concerns at the moment, as Aurelio had some major explaining to do.

Stella made coffee, and they all sat on kitchen island stools before Declan peered at Aurelio and asked tersely, "So, tell us about the gun—"

Aurelio clutched the mug, tasted the coffee and said unevenly, "Okay. Half an hour ago, my girlfriend, Bella Sorvino, and I were just talking inside my mom's Honda Prologue outside our house on Tutler's Way when this SUV drives past us. We didn't think anything of it, till the SUV stopped up ahead and a dude got out. He was carrying that—" Aurelio pointed to the bag on the island "—and walked over to a garbage can and tossed it inside, got back in his car and drove off like he was in a hurry."

Declan exchanged glances with Stella and asked him suspiciously, "You want to tell me how you ended up with the bag?"

Aurelio sipped more coffee nervously and answered, "Guess I was curious. While Bella waited in the car, I went to see what he had thrown away. That's when I saw the bag and took it out. I saw the gun inside and thought about tossing it back in the trash. But knowing you're with the KBI, when you're not knocking down shots in the park, I decided to bring it to you. Bella thought I should too."

Declan nodded. "Smart choice." He sipped coffee thoughtfully. "Did either of you touch the handgun?"

"Not a chance!" Aurelio made a face. "We weren't about to get our fingerprints on it and then have to explain that to you guys—knowing the dude probably had his reasons for getting rid of the gun..."

Stella smiled over her mug of coffee. "Another wise move by you and your girlfriend."

"Yeah," he muttered, putting the mug to his lips.

Declan agreed, giving them one less thing to deal with here if Aurelio and Bella were truly innocent of any wrongdoing—and he had to believe that was the case, considering that Aurelio was astute enough to bring the firearm to him.

He gazed at Aurelio and asked, "Can you describe this person you saw carrying the brown bag?"

"Definitely a white dude and tall. He was wearing dark clothes." Aurelio hunched broad shoulders. "Since it was nighttime, couldn't see his face when he turned our way for a second, but he didn't seem to see us. I think he had dark hair."

"What about the SUV he was driving?" Stella asked, sipping her coffee. "Can you describe it—make, model, color—anything would help..."

"Hmm...black, dark blue...something like that." Aurelio scratched his head. "It was too dark to get a good look at it before he took off."

Not surprising under the circumstances, Declan thought. "We'll see if any surveillance cameras near Tutler's Way can give us a more detailed description of the SUV during that timeframe."

Aurelio looked at him and asked grimly, "You think he shot someone with the gun?"

"That's a pretty good possibility," Declan answered logically. The question in his mind was whether or not it was the same Ronin Operator 9 mm pistol used by a serial killer who attempted another murder. "We may need to speak with your girlfriend later," he advised Aurelio, as standard procedure—even if Declan was certain he was on the level in his account.

Aurelio nodded. "Bella's kind of freaking out about it..." He paused. "Guess it has to do with her brother being accidentally shot while deployed with the US military in Syria."

"She has nothing to worry about," Declan tried to assure him. "We only want to get to the bottom of why someone chose to get rid of the gun—and in that location."

"Okay, I'll tell her that," he said.

Declan stood. "Thanks for bringing this to me. We'll take it from here."

Aurelio got to his feet. "Just doing my civic duty," he asserted.

"Good for you," Stella told him with a smile.

After Declan showed Aurelio out, he went back to Stella, who was examining the firearm inside the bag and asked him, "Do you think this is the handgun we've been looking for?"

He contemplated the question and responded with a gut feeling, "Probably. What better time for the unsub to get rid of the murder weapon and distance himself from it?"

"True." Stella finished her coffee. "We'll find out soon enough."

"Yep," Declan agreed, and was optimistic that it could be an important step toward the unsub's downfall. He gazed at her as his thoughts turned toward their being cozy in bed after hot sex, before Aurelio showed up. Now neither of them was likely to be getting much more sleep this night.

THE FOLLOWING AFTERNOON, Declan briefed the team on the latest development in the investigation. He made some general remarks, meant to offer a positive view that they were definitely on the right track in solving the case, and then asked forensic scientist Josephine Okamura to share her important news on the firearm brought to him by Aurelio Valderrama and turned over to the forensic science lab's Firearm and Toolmark Section for evaluation.

Josephine used a stylus pen to display a firearm on the large touch screen, as she said measuredly, "This Springfield Armory 1911 Ronin Operator 9 mm pistol armed with a sound suppressor, that Special Agent Delgado confiscated and sent to the evidence control center, proved to be a positive match for the bullets and spent shell casings linked to seven local murders and one attempted murder. Though the pistol was empty, a firearms examiner was able to test fire rounds to show that its gun barrel with six lands and grooves and a right-hand twist lined up perfectly with the bullets and casings involved in the homicides."

She took a short breath and said, "In other words, this is *definitely* the weapon used by the unsub referred to as the Bends Lake Predator to shoot the victims... The gun is still being processed for possible prints and DNA and has also been entered into the NIBIN to establish a link to any other crimes that might have been committed using the firearm—"

Declan offered her a smile and said, "Good job."

She nodded and said softly, "Hope you get him."

"You've put us on the right path," he told her. When she stepped away, Declan professed to the task force, "This was one of the things we've been waiting for to break this case wide open." He pointed at the Ronin Operator handgun still displayed on the monitor. "We have the murder weapon. And the bullets and shell casings fired from it. We also have the unsub on his heels, whether he knows it or not. Two teenagers spotted him getting rid of the handgun and saw the unsub drive off in a dark SUV, which corresponds with other info we have. We're currently collecting surveillance videos from the area that may help us to zoom in on the make and model of the SUV and identity of the driver—or, at the very least, a more accurate description. Until then, we need to remain diligent in our pursuit of the unsub so that he can't know a moment's rest from the chase..."

Declan let that settle in as Ursula said a few words, with Stella to follow in assessing the latest move—or blunder—by the Bends Lake Predator.

Stella wasted no time in giving them her honest impression of the unsub and his ridding himself of the primary piece of his killing machine puzzle—and what it may mean. She glanced at Declan and Ursula, then said to the team levelly, "Honestly, I believe that the unsub is running scared right now. By dumping the Springfield Armory 1911 Ronin Operator 9 mm pistol in the trash, it tells me that this was his way of trying to cut his losses, if you will, by separating himself from the handgun with which he was unable to kill his last target. In the process, the unsub may believe that this will somehow throw the investigators off track just enough to keep them at bay."

Keene Haverstock asked her, "So, are you saying that this is basically just a head fake on the part of the unsub and that he has every intention of carrying out more hits on targets, whether they're random or not?"

Good question, Stella told herself, and one she was fully prepared to respond to. She favored the FBI special agent with a serious look and responded bluntly, "I think it's highly likely that our unsub has no intention of fading into the woodwork. Like most serial killers, they fancy themselves as smarter than the rest of us. The Bends Lake Predator is no different." She furrowed her forehead and uttered ominously, "He will almost certainly strike again—with a new firearm and new prey—unless we can get to him first…"

Arielle Mendoza stated affirmatively, "That's why we're all here, right? It's what we do. We can't let him win. No matter his warped sense of self-importance."

"We won't," Declan stressed. "With the Ronin Operator handgun now safely in our possession, even if it's replaced by another weapon, the unsub has given us a major opening, and none of us will back down even a little bit until we make him pay for this—one way or another."

With this positive energy in the face of a relentless serial killer, Stella had to say, "Arielle's right. Whatever the unsub can do, we can do better. As I said, he's spooked right now, which, as Declan alluded to, can work to our advantage."

Stella eyed him and got a confident, if somewhat guarded, grin in return. She was glad to see that they were all on the same page in their renewed commitment toward bringing the Bends Lake Predator to his knees. She only wondered if and when other innocents might have to pay the ultimate price in the meantime.

AFTER THE BRIEFING was over, Declan drove to the basketball court, where he saw Aurelio shooting hoops alone. He wanted the teen to hear the news from him first on the gun he found.

After parking at the curb, Declan joined him on the court, still wearing his work clothing and shoes. Aurelio tossed the ball to him and said routinely, "Hey."

"Hey." Declan shot the ball flatfooted and drained it through the net. "Thought you might want to know about the firearm you brought me."

Aurelio dipped his chin. "Yeah. What did you find out?"

Meeting his gaze, Declan said straightforwardly, "The gun has been used in a string of local homicides."

"Seriously?" Aurelio raised a brow. "Are we talking about that serial killer on the loose…the Bends Lake Predator?"

"Yes, that's the person we believe the gun belonged to." Though Declan hated to lay this on him, he deserved to know the truth, given his inadvertent involvement in the investigation. "Needless to say, we're trying to locate the suspect and bring him in."

Aurelio tracked down the ball and asked warily, "So, am I—or Bella, for that matter—in any danger…?" He shot the ball, and it bounced off the rim. "I mean, I don't think the dude ever saw us." His eyes widened with realization. "But, oh man, what if he did? And now wants to come after us…?"

It was a valid question to Declan, and while he certainly couldn't rule out that the unsub could target Aurelio or Bella, it seemed like a low probability, all things considered. "My guess is that if the perp had spotted you and your girlfriend—and viewed you as a threat—you'd probably be dead right now," he said bluntly. Still, in erring on the side of caution, Declan told him, "You might want to play ball inside the gym for the time being."

"Okay." Aurelio dribbled the ball. "So, when are you going to catch this guy?"

Declan frowned. "I wish I could give you the answer to that, but I can't," he admitted, knowing that the investigation was ongoing and the unsub still out of their reach. "You can be sure, though, that all hands are on deck to capture him."

"All right." Aurelio clutched the ball to his chest.

"Come on, I'll give you a ride home," Declan said, as it was on the way to his own house and would allow him to make sure Aurelio got there safely.

Aurelio agreed, and during the ride, Declan surveyed other homes in the area and wondered if the unsub lived in any of them and in anonymity. His sense was that the Bends Lake Predator, being clever as he'd proven to be, had most likely driven a safe distance from his own residence. And chosen a spot at random to dump the handgun while hoping it would disappear forever. Along with his deadly association with it.

THE BENDS LAKE PREDATOR crouched among the sawtooth oak trees surrounding the single-track, three-mile loop trail. He had waited patiently and impatiently at the same time for his prey to arrive in his sights. Honestly, he was itching to pick up where he left off, now that he had discarded the 9 mm pistol and replaced it with another handgun that was equally lethal.

He thought back to when he had made the decision to trash the Ronin Operator gun. After failing to take out his last victim, he believed that the missed opportunity was bad karma. Not wishing to press his luck—or increase the luck of his prime targets—he made the smart move of relieving himself of the anvil that seemed to be weighing him down.

With that firearm dead and buried in the garbage and destined for a landfill, never to be seen again, he was now free to get back down to business. In throwing off his pursuers, he could start fresh as a killing machine and keep them guessing as to when, where and how his victims would be snuffed out like a candle.

It occurred to him that someone could have seen him when he tossed the gun in the garbage can. Had there been someone in that Honda he passed by? Or was that only his imagination?

In the end, he'd decided that it was too dark for anyone

to get a good look at him. Or his SUV. So he made haste and got the hell out of there. No harm. No foul. Right?

He sucked in a deep breath, enjoying the warm humid air. Not to mention the air of invincibility he had come to enjoy like a man who couldn't be touched.

The Bends Lake Predator's reverie stopped on a dime when he spotted two mountain bikes headed his way.

It's time, he told himself, cool as ice, as he stood erect but remained hidden till the very last moment. When escape would be all but impossible.

One error in judgment was enough. He wasn't about to let another golden opportunity slip through his grasp.

There would be two, this time around, who wouldn't come out of this alive.

He checked the gun, equipped with a silencer, and made sure that it was loaded and as ready as he was to do some serious damage to his unsuspecting victims.

Chapter Twelve

That morning, Ursula received a call that two people had been found dead on Bends Lake Trail, a zigzagging single-track trail popular among adventurers and exercisers for hiking and mountain biking. So what else was new? Still dealing with an ongoing case involving a ruthless serial killer, now it appeared as though the KBI would need to assist the locals in an entirely different investigation into what appeared to be homicides.

Unless there was some symmetry between the crimes? She considered the possibility that, as Stella had alluded to, the Bends Lake Predator had upped his game in preying upon others dramatically as his warped way of coming back with a vengeance after the failed attempt to murder Blake Michaud III.

Either way, it was the type of added stress that she didn't need. Not with a baby on the way. Even if Melody would be the one giving birth, Ursula was still in lockstep with her wife in going through the process. But she was also just as committed to her work in law enforcement.

I knew what I'd signed up for when I chose this career path, Ursula told herself as she drove the Chevrolet Malibu to Bends Lake Trail, right off Seemore Lane. She could only take whatever came her way—much like Declan and the other KBI special agents—and do her job.

When she arrived at the trail, Ursula showed her ID and was let past the cordoned-off crime scene, where she spotted Declan speaking with a Bends Lake PD homicide detective. Ursula recognized him as Zack Yamamoto, a tall and slender Japanese American in his late twenties with black hair in a curtain cut.

Looking beyond them, she saw a white male and a light-skinned biracial female lying on the ground. Their heads, with helmets on them, were surrounded by pools of blood. Both were slender and appeared to be in their thirties, wearing athletic attire and cycling shoes. Ursula regarded two mountain bikes on the ground, almost as if props. She knew that this was anything but the case as she approached the two men and geared herself up to face the music, melancholy as it was bound to be.

DECLAN FROWNED AS he peered at the dead man and woman, who had been identified as Trevor LeBlanc and Michelle Hewlett. They had been shot in cold blood at close range.

"No sign of a firearm to indicate a murder-suicide," Detective Zack Yamamoto told Ursula. "But there are spent shell casings on the ground." He ran a hand through his hair and grimaced. "Looks like they were ambushed..."

"By whom?" She wrinkled her nose. "Who would do such a horrible thing?"

"That's what we need to find out," Declan said tersely. "Given the angle of the wounds to the back of their heads, it appears as though the killer was lying in wait and was skillful enough to drop them from behind." He thought about the Bends Lake Predator, wondering if he was sharp enough to change his tactics to this degree. Declan imagined that Stella would have some thoughts on it when she learned the unsettling news. But as of now, they had to keep an open mind that the cyclists may have had enemies that were only after them, and therefore could be totally separate from their serial killer investigation.

Zack, who was looking at his cell phone, said, "I may have something on that…" He got between Declan and Ursula. "A hiker named Josette Edmonds has come forward, saying she saw a strange man running from the area. Without knowing if he was running from something, instinctively, she used her cell phone video to capture him before he disappeared into a wooded area. With the press already reporting on the fatal shooting, Ms. Edmonds has sent us the video she took. Here it is…"

Declan watched as a tall and fit white male, wearing dark clothing and a hoodie with the hood over his head, dashed through the woods like a roadrunner before vanishing from sight.

"Hmm…" Ursula uttered musingly, turning to him. "Are you thinking what I'm thinking?"

"How could I not be?" Declan answered honestly. "The general physical characteristics look an awful lot like those of the Bends Lake Predator—"

When the medical examiner arrived and a preliminary examination indicated the point-blank range execution of the man and woman, Declan hoped that the crime scene investigators could come up with damning evidence in the pursuit of justice. Though he wasn't ruling out that the victims could have been targeted specifically for the kill, Declan had a feeling that this was the work of a serial killer run amok.

FOUR HOURS LATER, Declan sat in his car. He had learned that Michelle Hewlett and Trevor LeBlanc were Canadians, staying at a log cabin near Bends Lake Trail. They had only been there for three days, having flown in from Winnipeg, Manitoba, to Great Bend, Kansas, where the couple rented a GMC Yukon for a weeklong adventure.

One that ended tragically.

Declan saw no evidence that it was a robbery gone bad, as all their belongings were still inside the cabin. Nor was there any indication that the couple had been otherwise targeted by someone from their hometown, following them to Kansas in order to commit cold-blooded murder.

As far as he could tell, Declan believed that Hewlett and LeBlanc may have been chosen randomly to be killed—though, the culprit could have tracked their pattern of apparently riding their mountain bikes at the same time every day.

That, along with the video of an unsub running away from the scene, gives more credence to this being the work of their serial killer, Declan told himself as he opened his laptop. The changing modus operandi notwithstanding—with the victims each shot twice in the back of the head—it had all the indications of thrill killings, which seemed to reflect the mindset of the serial killer at large.

He reached out to the Firearm and Toolmark Section

of the forensic science lab to get the scoop on the bullets and shell casings used in the double homicide.

When Josephine Okamura appeared on the screen, she smiled softly as Declan said, "What do you have for me?"

She was all business as she brought him up to speed on the news he sought, finishing with an edge to her voice, "So there you have it."

"Indeed, and thanks," he told her and disconnected before starting the car and heading for another important briefing.

In the conference room, where Declan had reconvened the team for the second time in two days, he went right to the heart of the matter. Using the stylus pen, he put the images of the victims of the double homicide side by side on the screen and said soberly, "Sometime this morning, Michelle Hewlett, a thirty-three-year-old veterinarian, and Trevor LeBlanc, a thirty-seven-year-old dentist, were gunned down while riding mountain bikes on the Bends Lake Trail loop."

Declan paused while gazing at Hewlett, who was nice-looking with a black wavy bob and big brown eyes; then he turned to LeBlanc, who was square-jawed with blue eyes and blond hair in a pompadour style. "The two Canadian adventurers were vacationing in Kansas, with plans to travel to Tennessee to visit the Great Smoky Mountains National Park next on their agenda—when it appears they were ambushed by the killer, who shot both victims twice in the back of the head."

Flipping to an image of a firearm, Declan said, "According to ballistics, the four bullets used to shoot the pair and spent shell casings came from a Taurus GX4 9 mm Luger pistol—like the one shown on the screen—

with a gun barrel that has five lands and grooves and a left-hand twist." He took a breath and continued, "We have reason to believe that the shooter may be the same unsub responsible for the shooting deaths of seven other individuals and the attempted murder of a man."

Declan played a video while explaining, "This video was shot by a hiker shortly after the murders were believed to have occurred. It shows an unsub who shares characteristics of the Bends Lake Predator suspect—" He turned off the monitor. "The change of tactics is likely a maneuver borne out of necessity. Or to throw us off guard in believing we're dealing with an entirely different killer. Though all possibilities remain on the table, my current thinking is that we are dealing with the same unsub…"

After Declan turned it over to Detective Zack Yamamoto to give a few more details on the police department's investigation, Stella took to the podium to reiterate her stance on the unsub and the propensity for altering his modus operandi.

She eyed Declan, and he flashed her a show of support as Stella said smoothly, "The double homicide probe is just getting started—and could well be the work of a separate murderer. As we all know, there are many people capable of committing such violent acts in our society. I tend to concur with Declan that there is a strong possibility that the murders of these two individuals were perpetrated by the so-called Bends Lake Predator."

Stella brushed aside a strand of hair that had fallen onto her face and continued, "A killer's MO is never set in stone. Yes, there tends to be predictable patterns of behavior, but this is always subject to change as conditions warrant. In this instance, the use of a Taurus GX4 9 mm Luger pistol rather than another Springfield Armory 1911 Ronin Operator 9 mm handgun may be as simple as accessibility for the unsub. And choosing to shoot them both twice in the head, instead of once in the head and two other times in the chest or stomach, may be little more than a strategic move to confound the authorities—with the unsub confident in achieving the intended result of killing the victims."

She sighed and said, "Lastly, murdering two for the price of one may well have been a make-up murder, if you will—an extra murder to take the place of the missed opportunity in the attempted murder of Blake Michaud III. In the unsub's warped mind, he feels the need to be in control of all aspects of his serial actions—even to the point of satisfying his homicidal impulses with a substitute killing, in addition to the preplanned murder of someone who happened to come into his line of vision."

THAT EVENING, Stella and Declan joined a few other members of the team at Hedy's Club, where they sat around a table, drinking beer.

Declan wiped froth from his mouth and said tonelessly, "Never a dull day in our line of work."

Keene Haverstock nodded, then added sardonically, "What fun would that be?" He added on a serious note, "Not that there's anything fun about nine people dead and a tenth person who's damned lucky to be alive."

Declan drank more beer. "Tell me about it."

"If it turns out to be true that Michelle Hewlett and Trevor LeBlanc were killed by a serial killer, then this unsub is some piece of work," Zack Yamamoto remarked.

"I'd say that's putting it mildly," Arielle Mendoza said, lifting her mug. "I wouldn't necessarily say that he's a psychopath, but he's definitely playing his hand with a deranged mindset, if you ask me. Or maybe I should defer to our visiting behavioral analyst…"

Stella smiled, tasting her drink while feeling all eyes on her, as though she could provide easy answers for why one becomes a serial killer. If only it was that simple. She would try to make some sense of it anyhow. "I'll give it a shot," she told them lightheartedly. "Our unsub is definitely a deviant, which I'm sure we all agree with, and is likely a psychopath. As it relates to psychopathy, which correlates on many levels with sociopathy—I'll just say that both are antisocial personality disorders that tend to be characterized by arrogance, no value for human life other than one's own, having little to no remorse for the criminal behavior and getting turned on by the power wielded in creating fear and helplessness among victims." Stella chuckled, feeling a bit embarrassed. "I think I probably said too much—I'm boring everyone to tears."

Declan smiled. "I wouldn't go that far," he said sincerely. "Your insight has been evident since you got to town. It's done wonders to give us some perspective while trying to deal with this monster."

"I'm totally with Declan there," Keene said, drinking beer. "Guess that's why the Bureau pays you the big bucks, Stella."

Arielle joked, "Actually, I think those come more from the royalties from her books."

Stella blushed and laughed. "Will you guys stop it? I'm just doing my job like everyone else. But I wouldn't trade it for anything." She gazed at Declan, who stared back at her, and in that moment thought, *Except for maybe finding true love and settling down into a lasting relationship and happy home.* She wondered if that was forthcoming. Or had that ship already sailed past her?

"IT'S BEEN REALLY nice having you here," Declan told Stella that night.

"Oh, really?" She chuckled. "Bet you say that to every naked criminal profiler you have in your bed."

Now he laughed. "Not quite," he professed. "Haven't had any other profilers in here. And wouldn't want any. You're a hard act to follow, Stella. Trust me when I say that."

She looked him in the eye with a straight face and said, "Actually, I think I do trust you…and whatever it is that's happening here—"

"Good." He held her gaze with sincerity. "I feel the same way."

"And what way is that?" she challenged him.

Declan froze. Not because he was at a loss for words. Quite the contrary. He knew precisely what he felt in his heart and soul for her. She had come back into his life at just the right time—and given him a whole new reason to believe in love again. And a future. Where the problem came in was exactly how they could navigate that future, given the different trajectories of their lives and careers at the moment. Could they meet somewhere in the middle? Or would they only wind up repeating the mistakes of the past? And in the process lose everything they could have in the precious years ahead?

"What's the matter?" Stella broke through his reverie, an uneasy catch to her tone. "Cat got your tongue?"

Declan grinned crookedly, realizing he needed to give her something that let Stella know in clear language that he was in this for the long run—without getting too far ahead of himself. Or beyond her own comfort level, as they both lay naked in bed.

Declan breathed in air and said deliberately, "What I'm trying to say is that you can count on me to be there for you—and to not allow this bond we've established or reestablished, if you will, to slip away again." He paused. "Once we get past this investigation and can put all the focus on us, we can delve deeper into where we are and where we go from here—" *I hope that will suffice for now*, he told himself as they cuddled.

"All right." Stella's voice was soft. Her body even softer. "We'll do this your way."

Declan was pleased that she was amenable to allowing things to play themselves out, with a positive outcome something they both strove for in the end. He held her even closer, kissing the side of Stella's head and then her bare shoulder while deep in thought.

Chapter Thirteen

When the KBI received a call the following day from someone indicating they might have important information about the murder of Diane Wexler, Declan was quick to check it out, wanting to leave no stone unturned in solving the crime. The caller, who identified herself as Gillian Estrada, was said to be a good friend of Diane's.

He drove to a posh two-story residence on Lavador Lane and parked behind a yellow BMW M2 Coupe before heading up to the house.

The front door opened when he reached the covered porch. Standing before him was a striking, well-dressed, slender Hispanic female in her early fifties, with shoulder-length layered curly hair and hazel eyes behind heart-shaped glasses.

"I'm Gillian Estrada," she said softly.

"Special Agent Delgado."

"Thank you for coming." She shook his hand and told him, "Please come in."

Declan followed her inside. Similar to Diane Wexler's nearby residence, it exuded the trappings of wealth with mahogany handcrafted furniture on beige hybrid flooring and numerous floor-to-ceiling windows. A Siamese cat strode across the floor nonchalantly.

Declan gazed at the homeowner and asked curiously, "You mentioned that you may have some relevant information on the Diane Wexler homicide investigation?"

"Yes..." She touched her glasses nervously. "Mind if we sit down?"

"Not at all." He sat on a blue armchair and watched her do the same.

Gillian clasped her hands and, after taking a moment, uttered, "I was devastated to hear about Diane's death. Was on a cruise when it happened and didn't receive the news until I got home."

"So, you two were close?" Declan asked, remembering that she had indicated as much.

"Yes, we hung out, when afforded the time to do so. But since she was married—if not always happily—and I was definitely happy as a divorcée, there was that getting in the way." When the cat jumped up on her lap, Gillian petted it and said thoughtfully, "Diane and I attended a fundraiser about three months ago. There was a guy who worked for the firm that provided security services who tried to hit on Diane. She politely rebuffed his efforts, but he still seemed to take it the wrong way. Honestly, it was creepy." Gillian took a breath and let the cat go. "Maybe it ended there—Diane never indicated otherwise—but after learning that she had been murdered, possibly by a serial killer, this man came to mind as someone I wanted to bring to your attention...just in case—"

Declan reacted with interest. "I'm glad you did," he told her. "Did you or Diane happen to get this man's name?"

"I think it was Sam," Gillian said.

Sam is a pretty common name, Declan thought, but it

was still worth checking out. "Can you narrow it down to exactly when and where the fundraiser took place?"

She nodded. "I can get that information for you."

"Okay." He regarded the cat that had jumped back on her lap. "If there's anything that can connect this Sam to Diane's death, we'll find out."

Gillian said, "Thank you. Diane was such a gentle soul. She didn't deserve to be taken away like that—leaving behind her daughter and husband."

"I couldn't agree more," Declan concurred, reminded of the tragic loss of his own wife prematurely. Even as he had to come to terms with the strong feelings he now—and probably always, if the truth be told—had for her sister. He felt blessed to have had them both in his life at the right times.

DECLAN AND KEENE walked into the McIntosh Security Agency on Rottenham Road and approached the front desk in the small lobby.

Standing in front of a computer on a granite counter was a sixtysomething lean man with fine slicked-back white hair and a matching horseshoe-shaped mustache. He eyed them behind round glasses and asked, "Can I help you?"

After they identified themselves, Keene said, "And you are?"

"Vince McIntosh. I own the agency."

Declan said, "We need some information on one of your employees who was on hand three months ago at a fundraiser in a building on Kayllen Avenue."

"Okay." Vince regarded them for a moment. "What does this pertain to?"

"It's a murder investigation," Keene said sharply.

"Murder?" Vince flashed a look of shock. "Of who?"

"We'd rather not say for the time being," Declan told him, preferring to limit what they divulged while probing into one of his personnel.

With a frown on his face, Vince asked, "What's the name of the employee?"

"We only have Sam to go with," Declan answered, hoping that would be enough.

"The only Sam we had on the payroll then as an armed security guard that would've been at the fundraiser was Samuel O'Shea," Vince said matter-of-factly.

Keene peered at him. "You said, 'had on the payroll'?"

"Yes. We let him go a couple of months ago, after receiving complaints from some of our clients of harassment and other behavior inconsistent with company standards," Vince explained, jutting his chin.

That sounds about right, Declan mused, considering Gillian Estrada's account of a man named Sam who stepped outside the line in pursuing Diane Wexler's affections, to no avail. But did this amount to murder? Not to mention a notch on the belt of a serial killer?

Declan regarded the security agency owner and asked intently, "So, what does this Samuel O'Shea look like?"

"Let me pull up his data," Vince said, and began typing on the computer's keyboard.

Within moments, he had printed out an image of Samuel O'Shea. Declan and Keene studied it. The thirty-eight-year-old former security guard was listed at six feet, three inches tall and had short dark hair, a square face and blue eyes. He seemed to fit the general characteristics of the unsub they were after in the string of murders, which merited moving forward in speaking with O'Shea as a suspect.

"We need an address for Samuel O'Shea," Keene said, peering at Vince.

"No problem," he responded, but added defensively, "There were no red flags in Sam's background check." Vince sucked in a deep breath. "I hope you're on the wrong track here."

"Only time will tell," Declan said straightforwardly. Even if there was no criminal record, he had a sense that O'Shea was a legitimate person of interest and asked, "What model of handguns do your security officers carry?"

"We're equipped with Ruger LC9 semiautomatic pistols," Vince answered tonelessly. "Why do you ask?"

Because I wanted to see if they were Springfield Armory 1911 Ronin Operator 9 mm pistols, Declan thought, *like the one used by the unsub in Diane Wexler's murder.* He said, though, "Just a routine part of the inquiry."

Vince nodded and handed them Samuel O'Shea's last known address, before they headed out of the security agency.

"So, what do you think?" Keene asked once they stepped outside, his jaw set. "Would this guy truly carry a grudge for three months after being snubbed—leading to murder? Not to mention the other murders tied to the unsub?"

"Why not?" Declan answered thoughtfully. "Who's to say the victims weren't all targeted because of some real or imagined snubbing or related in some way vendetta? Beyond that, the unsub could well have used some of the other killings as a smokescreen—with Diane Wexler being his primary target." *Or maybe I'm stretching the scenarios too far and wide*, Declan mused, as he second-guessed himself, while keeping open the possibilities.

"Point taken," Keene said. "Let's go pay Samuel O'Shea a visit and see what he has to say about this."

Declan nodded pensively as they headed toward his vehicle.

STELLA JOGGED ACROSS the grass on Declan's property while admiring the view of the Cheyenne Bottoms wetland and migrating birds. She was envious that he got to enjoy this amazing wetland year-round, as well as visit the nearby Quivira National Wildlife Refuge whenever afforded the time.

Yes, I suppose I could get used to this in a hurry, Stella told herself while moving at a leisurely pace. Just as Elise had when it was her time to be with Declan. But her sister was in a different place now. *And I'm still here, looking for the same things in life: love and happiness*, she thought.

Stella was sure that Declan felt the same way. And he had intimated that they were on the same page where it concerned their affections for each other. Even if the word *love* had yet to be spoken out loud by either of them. But it seemed like this was a mere formality that they would confront once the serial killer case had run its course.

I have to exercise patience till then, Stella told herself, having had years of practice doing just that. Still of concern to her, though, was the reality that she had a life—and parents—in Detroit. Not to mention, the demands of her profession that could take her far away from home at a moment's notice.

So deal with it when the time comes, she thought with determination, not wanting to let the possibilities of a solid relationship pass her by once more.

When she got back to the house and did her cool down, Stella drank a bottle of water and then called her parents. It seemed like a good idea to inform them of where things stood between her and Declan these days.

"Hey," she said cheerfully when they both appeared on the cell phone screen.

"Hi, Stella." Her mother smiled brightly. "Nice hearing from you, as always."

"Hi, honey," her father said evenly. "How's the investigation going?"

Stella filled them in, stressing that it was still ongoing, but they were making progress to some degree. They understood that these complex cases took time to unwind, unlike in a police procedural movie. But still, her parents wondered when she might be coming home to Detroit, where they liked to get together at least once a week for a family dinner.

After a moment or two, Stella gazed at them and said in a calm voice, "So, I've started seeing Declan…"

Lester Bailey cocked a brow. "Really?"

"Yes," she reiterated. "We talked and smoothed things out. The rest just fell into place."

Ngozi Bailey put a big grin on her face and declared, "Well, it's about time. You two have obviously been connected for years. There's nothing wrong with that. Elise would definitely choose you to make Declan happy, if she could no longer be around to do so."

"I agree," her father said, nodding with approval.

Stella's eyes lit up. "Thank you both." She was delighted to have their support. Now came the harder part. "I'm not sure how this will work out as far as my job and what the future holds. I'll just have to go with the flow and see what happens."

Her father said, "We understand. Do what's best for you—and Declan. We only want you to be comfortable with whatever decisions you make, honey, and we'll always be with you, geography aside."

"Absolutely," her mother concurred.

"Love you guys," Stella uttered, nearly brought to tears, while counting her blessings for having them in her life.

After disconnecting, she gave her boss, Valerie, a call to update her on the latest news with respect to the Bends Lake Predator case. Then Stella sat on a stool at the kitchen island and opened her laptop. She looked at the proposal she had been working on for her next series of books—apart from having one more book currently under contract—while hoping her agent would approve, even while pondering how to best balance her work and private life looking ahead.

DECLAN AND KEENE walked onto the porch of a single-story ranch-style home on Zeldon Road, hoping to have a word with Samuel O'Shea.

Declan took note of the maroon Volvo XC60 parked in the driveway, after having established that a black Cadillac Escalade SUV was registered under the name of Samuel L. O'Shea.

When the front door of the house opened, a slender

Native American woman, perhaps in her seventies, with a gray pixie and wearing round glasses, stood there. She asked simply, "What do you want?"

After flashing his ID, Declan responded, "We're looking for Samuel O'Shea."

"He doesn't live here anymore," she said succinctly.

"And you are?" Keene asked her.

"Mary Arbuckle."

He peered at her. "We have O'Shea living at this address."

Mary batted her eyes. "I bought this house two months ago…and don't have a forwarding address for him." Her eyes shifted between them. "Feel free to look around inside, if you want."

Declan considered this, but made a judgement call that O'Shea had moved, for whatever reason, after being canned by the security agency. But to where? And could this have anything to do with his harassment of Diane Wexler? Or even more ominous reasons—such as staying on the move as a serial killer?

"That won't be necessary," Declan told her with an affable grin. "Thank you for your time."

As they headed from the house, Keene asked, "What are you thinking about O'Shea?"

Declan responded candidly, "I'm thinking we need to talk to him—and fast! If O'Shea is indeed our unsub in the murder of Diane Wexler—along with the other related homicides—there's no telling what he may do next. And to whom…"

"I'm with you there." Keene ran a hand through his hair. "The unsub—maybe O'Shea—has seemingly been steps ahead of us with each killing. It's time we gain some serious ground here…"

"Yeah, it's way overdue," Declan said firmly, as they tried to step it up a gear in pursuit of the latest person of interest.

An hour later, Declan was at his desk at the field office, still digesting the case's various and often typical twists and turns, when he got a video call request from the KBI's forensic science laboratory technician, Ike Osorno. Accepting the call, Declan watched as his face appeared. Ike, who was in his midthirties, had red hair in a brush cut and a goatee.

"What's up?" Declan asked.

With a deadpan look, Ike said, "About the Diane Wexler murder, I have some news for you." He paused. "The Crime Scene Response Team was able to pull a latent print from near the sliding back door."

"Okay…" Declan uttered impatiently.

"We ran it through the FBI's Next Generation Identification system's Advanced Fingerprint Identification Technology and got a hit!" Ike's face lit up with enthusiasm. "It came back with the name Samuel L. O'Shea."

"O'Shea?" Declan was thinking out loud as the name smacked at him like a slap in the face, along with the fact that he'd already been someone they were currently looking into as a person of interest.

"Yeah," Ike said. "Looks like this Samuel L. O'Shea has a lot of explaining to do."

"I have a feeling it's not something he'll be able to talk his way out of," Declan declared. Especially when piecing together some of the assorted parts of the puzzle. Not the least of which was Diane's expressed concerns about the former security guard. And apparently for good reason. "Good job, Ike."

"Thanks." He grinned. "Bring him in."

"We definitely intend to," Declan assured him, and thought, *But first we need to locate the suspect.*

After he ended the chat, an arrest warrant was issued for Samuel L. O'Shea, who, unless it was somehow proven otherwise, had to be considered armed and dangerous.

Chapter Fourteen

"I've seen this face before," Stella uttered with a decided edge to her voice, as she stared at the printout Declan brought home of the man suspected in the death of Diane Wexler, as well as the string of other murders.

"You have?" Declan regarded her. "Where?"

"At least, I think I have," she said, studying the image of Samuel O'Shea further as second thoughts crept into her head like a migraine. "He looks an awful lot like my high school friend Gayle Reese's cousin, Lochlyn—minus the stubble beard he had on his face. We met briefly at the gift shop in the hotel on the day I checked out." She took a breath, hating to think that someone in Gayle's family could, in fact, be a killer. Much less, a serial killer. But then again, stranger things had happened. Stella knew from experience as a criminal profiler that anyone was capable of anything—even while presenting a normal facade.

"Hmm..." Declan jutted his chin as they stood in the great room. "His name is actually Samuel L. O'Shea. The *L* could be short for Lochlyn."

Stella agreed and said intuitively, "It probably is."

"Did you learn anything about him?"

"Not really," she said regrettably. "Only that he attended and graduated from Bends Lake High School years before I did. And likes to play tennis."

"He may also have a predilection for serial murder," Declan voiced ominously, "if this Lochlyn and Samuel L. O'Shea are one and the same—and currently at large and wanted as a person of interest in at least one homicide. I think we need to pay your high school friend a visit and see what she has to say about her cousin...and depending on that, where he might be located—"

Stella nodded. "All right." Hard as it was to have to confront Gayle about this, it was so much harder to know that a homicidal predator was running loose and, most likely, still hunting for victims.

WHEN THEY WALKED inside the gift shop, Declan took note of the attractive female behind the counter, with long blond balayage hair, as Stella had described her old high school chum, and wearing horn-rimmed eyeglasses. Were she and the suspect related? If so, Declan had to wonder if she had been privy to Samuel L. O'Shea's wrongdoings. And whether she had been covering for him, to her own detriment.

Gayle looked up as they approached her and, after smiling at Stella, said evenly, "Hey. Thought you'd left town?"

"Not quite." Stella glanced at Declan and then gave her a poker-faced look. "I actually only moved out of the hotel."

"I see." Gayle looked from one to the other and asked her, "So, what's up?"

Stella responded seriously, "This is KBI special agent

Declan Delgado. If you have a moment, he has some questions for you."

And if you don't have a moment, you'll have no choice but to make one, Declan thought surely, as Gayle said, ill at ease, "Uh, okay. What questions…?"

Declan pulled the printout of Samuel L. O'Shea from the pocket of his navy wool blazer and showed it to her as he asked straightforwardly, "Do you recognize this man?"

After pushing her glasses up, Gayle studied the picture for a beat then answered, "Yes, it looks like my cousin Lochlyn…" She turned to Stella and asked, "What's this about?"

Stella blinked and responded coolly, "Is Lochlyn's full name Samuel L. O'Shea?"

Gayle nodded. "He's always gone by his middle name, Lochlyn. At least with family and friends." Her voice shook. "What has he done…?"

Declan took over from there, sparing Stella from having to spill the beans. He said flatly, "O'Shea is suspected of murdering a woman named Diane Wexler…"

Gayle's eyes widened. "What?"

After repeating the gist of his words, Declan told her, pulling no punches, "Your cousin is in big trouble. Apart from that murder, we believe he may also be responsible for a number of other homicides perpetrated by a man with the nickname the Bends Lake Predator—"

Gayle put a hand to her mouth in disbelief and shook her head. "It can't be."

"We hope you're right about that," Stella told her gently. "Which is why we need to bring Lochlyn in and see how he responds to the accusations."

Declan said, "O'Shea no longer lives at the address his former employer gave us on Zeldon Road." He peered at her. "Do you know where he's currently staying?"

"I didn't realize he'd lost his job." Gayle frowned and her voice lowered an octave as reality seemed to set in. "Lochlyn's been living in a mobile home on Pletcher Road for the last two months."

Declan reacted to the street name and asked, "That wouldn't happen to be the Wylson Mobile Home Park, would it?"

"Yes, that's the one," she responded without hesitation.

It quickly came to Declan's mind that it was the same mobile home park where a previous suspect in the serial killer investigation, Joaquin Kalember, lived. What were the odds? Might the two be in cahoots?

Declan recalled that Kalember's alibi had held up in the attempted murder of Blake Michaud III. And though Kalember was charged with possessing child porn and illicit drugs, he had been dropped as a suspect in the Bends Lake Predator case.

Whether that was premature or not remains to be seen, Declan told himself. He fixed Gayle's face and said warningly, "It wouldn't be very smart of you to tip off O'Shea that we're coming after him. That's called obstruction of justice or accessory after the fact. Take your pick."

Gayle grimaced. "I'm not about to interfere in your investigation, Agent Delgado," she insisted.

"Good." For now, Declan was willing to give her the benefit of the doubt that she played no role in the suspected criminality by her cousin. Relatives were often the last to know what killers had been up to, when uninvolved themselves.

Gayle gazed at Stella and said firmly, "If Lochlyn is guilty, he needs to answer for it."

Stella nodded. "Sorry about this."

"Me too," she told her, voice cracking.

Declan was sorry as well—but for the victims of a serial killer and anyone else who could still find themselves in his crosshairs.

THE SUSPECT'S SUV was nowhere to be found in the Wylson Mobile Home Park, and there was no indication that Samuel L. O'Shea was inside his manufactured home as it was surrounded by a KBI Special Operations Division's High Risk Warrant Team, an FBI Special Weapons and Tactics team, Danver County Sheriff's Office's Criminal Investigations Division detectives, and the Bends Lake Police Department K-9 unit.

In advance, knowing that O'Shea might be on the move, Declan had obtained a warrant to search the premises, making sure they were doing everything by the book. He was hoping to find any additional evidence to link the suspect to Diane Wexler's murder or any of the other homicides tied to their serial killer.

With no response from inside, Declan eyed Ursula, then in a case of déjà vu, he gave the nod to go into the mobile home by force. He had his SIG Sauer P226 9 mm semiautomatic pistol out and was wearing a tactical vest for protection in case of an ambush. They stormed the place, using a battering ram to enter the premises.

There was no one present inside the brown-carpeted, sparsely furnished, two-bedroom home—but they found a stockpile of weapons and ammunition. Among the firearms was a Mossberg MC2sc Optic-Ready 9 mm pistol, a Smith & Wesson CSX 9 mm pistol, and a Military Armament Corporation 1911 Double Stack 9 mm handgun. Rifles confiscated included a Sauer 505 Synchro XT bolt-action rifle, a Beretta BRX1 bolt-action rifle and a Mossberg Patriot Predator SF rifle.

"Seems like O'Shea was preparing for war," remarked KBI special agent Noah Rudd, a tall thirtysomething African American man with a black flattop hairstyle.

"Yeah, I can see that," Declan had to agree as they went through the place, which based on the disarray, appeared as if O'Shea had left in a hurry. Had he been given a heads-up that they were coming his way? Or was it more instinctive for the suspected killer to be wary at every turn in how he operated and came and went—for obvious reasons? Until proven to the contrary, Declan decided that Gayle hadn't gone against her word in warning her cousin that they were onto him and in hot pursuit.

"Look what we have here," Ursula said, walking into the room. Wearing a nitrile glove, she was holding a firearm. "A Taurus GX4 9 mm Luger pistol...complete with a sound suppressor—"

Declan raised a brow and said matter-of-factly, "Like the one used to shoot to death Michelle Hewlett and Trevor LeBlanc."

"My thinking precisely," she agreed, and plopped the weapon in an evidence bag. "Let's see what ballistics has to say about it."

"In the meantime, there's no reason to believe that O'Shea isn't still packing with another firearm from his arsenal," Declan told her astutely. "Making him just as serious a threat to the public as before till we can bring O'Shea in."

Ursula bobbed her head. "Right."

A BOLO alert was issued for Samuel L. O'Shea, who was considered armed and dangerous, and the black Cadillac Escalade SUV he was believed to be driving.

Declan could only hope they could get to him before anyone else had to die.

STELLA WAS STILL reeling over the notion that Gayle Reese's cousin Lochlyn—aka Samuel L. O'Shea—was now the number one suspect in a string of deaths. Though she didn't know Gayle all that well, Stella honestly believed that her high school classmate had no knowledge of O'Shea doubling as a serial killer in their midst.

Not exactly the type of secret you keep to yourself in order to protect a cousin—at the risk of being dragged into the investigation as an accomplice to taking the lives of others, Stella thought as she sat alongside Declan in his Chevrolet Malibu. He was silent with his own thoughts as the case was heating up following the raid on O'Shea's mobile home that turned up possible evidence to implicate him in one or more homicides.

They were en route to Bends Lake Hospital, where the lone survivor of the Bends Lake Predator, Blake Michaud III, was still recovering from his serious injuries. But felt well enough that he requested a meeting with investigators on the case.

Stella was curious as to what he had to say, after the description he'd given of his attacker proved to be incorrect, though it was understandable, given his state at the time and the stress he was under.

Declan broke the silence when he said from behind the wheel, "We'll get through this, you know…?"

She wondered if he was referring to the investigation or the ups and downs of their relationship. Both seemed apropos to her. She nodded. "I know."

He flashed her a slight smile. "We make a great team—whichever sport you choose."

She couldn't help but smile at the sports metaphor. "You think?"

Touching her hand with his free hand, he said prophetically, "Wait and see."

"I will," she promised, taking him at his word that better days were ahead, once this was all behind them.

After arriving at the hospital, they went to Blake Michaud's room and found him sitting on an armchair, eating ice cream. Stella imagined that he looked much better than the last time Declan had visited him.

"This is Special Agent Bailey," Declan introduced her, after reiterating his own identification.

"Thanks for coming," Blake said, looking from one to the other as he put the ice cream bowl on a table.

Nodding, Declan asked him, "How are you feeling?"

"Better than the last time you were here. Doctors tell me I'll be released this week. I'm counting the minutes till that happens so I can get back to my life."

"Good." Declan tilted his head. "Do you have new information to share?"

"Yeah," Blake answered thoughtfully. "I heard that you have a new suspect in the case?"

Declan confirmed, "We do."

"I saw his picture on the TV screen." Blake shifted in

the chair. "It was him—Samuel O'Shea—the guy who shot me—"

Declan glanced at Stella and back to him keenly. "You're sure about that?"

"Yes, I'm sure," Blake replied without prelude. "I know my initial description of the attacker was off. But I was under medication and somewhat disoriented at the time—and wasn't able to think clearly."

"And you can now?" Stella questioned him.

"Yeah. I've had nothing but time to go over it—him—in my head. That's the face—and the eyes—I saw... He's the one who shot me and left me for dead!"

"Okay," Declan told him. "That's helpful to the investigation."

Stella felt the same and asked curiously, "Had you ever seen the shooter before the encounter...?"

Blake stared at the question for a long moment, then responded contemplatively, "It's possible—but no time, in particular, comes to mind."

She considered if O'Shea could have stalked him for whatever reason as a target—before shooting him with the clear intent to kill. Or was the victim, like apparently most of the others, simply at the wrong place at the wrong time?

Declan squared his shoulders and told him, "If anything else comes to mind about your attacker, let us know."

"I will." Blake drew his brows together. "Hope you get the creep—before anyone else has to go through what I have."

"I understand where you're coming from," Declan said sincerely.

Stella added, "We both do." He may have been the lucky one, in comparison to the other victims of the Bends Lake Predator, but she knew that survivor's guilt—or survivor syndrome—was a real affliction as a facet of post-traumatic stress disorder. And a serious burden, in and of itself, for anyone who walked away from a serial killer. She hoped Blake would get the treatment he would need to deal with it, once released.

In the interim, he had provided them with another important piece of the puzzle in pointing the finger at Samuel L. O'Shea as the Bends Lake Predator.

Chapter Fifteen

The next morning, Declan sat at his desk in the field office, assessing the information they had on the still-at-large suspect, Samuel O'Shea. There were plenty of reasons to believe that he was the serial killer they were trying to capture. O'Shea had managed to evade them through clever maneuvers, handpicking victims when most vulnerable and likely with a preplanned escape route, skillful circumventing of solid evidence to tie him to the crimes and just plain old luck that worked to his benefit.

But your luck's about to run out, O'Shea, Declan told himself, feeling as certain of that as he had in the investigation up to this point. They would soon have the elusive predator in custody. But soon couldn't come soon enough.

Especially when Declan would much rather be focused on Stella and just how far they could go from here, if both were willing to let down their barriers against getting hurt. He had a good feeling that this was well within their capabilities—and a strong desire to build something special together.

Refocusing on the matter at hand, Declan looked at his laptop and did a deep dive on Samuel O'Shea to see what made him tick, to the extent that this was possible. He saw that O'Shea had a checkered past as far as his employment history, having worked in construction, sales, wilderness-related jobs and, most recently, security. He'd been married once, to Tonya O'Shea, though it ended in divorce three years ago after an apparently contentious relationship between them. The ex-wife had since remarried and relocated to the Big Island of Hawaii.

Declan took note of O'Shea's stockpile of weapons, some of which had been legally purchased. Others were illegally owned firearms. The latter included those he was suspected to be using to perpetrate serial homicides.

I wonder what handgun he's carrying at the moment, Declan contemplated with concern, fearing the suspect could use it before being located and taken into custody.

After conferring with Kimberly Ullerich, the special agent in charge, and getting her full support, he convened the task force for an important update on where things stood in the investigation.

Standing at the front of the conference room, Declan lifted the stylus pen and turned to the touch screen display. He put O'Shea's image on the monitor and said measuredly, "Thirty-eight-year-old Samuel Lochlyn O'Shea, a former security guard, has emerged as our chief suspect in the Bends Lake Predator investigation. Between raiding his mobile home and coming away with crucial evidence and other key evidence that's come to light, it's pretty apparent that O'Shea is the serial killer we're after—"

Declan talked a bit more about this and then turned it over to forensic technician Ike Osorno, who scratched his goatee and said evenly, "We were able to collect a

DNA sample from the top of the trash can on Tutler's Way, where the Springfield Armory 1911 Ronin Operator 9 mm handgun linked to the Bends Lake Predator was discovered. The sample was put into the Federal DNA Database Unit's National DNA Index System as part of CODIS. It was initially an unknown forensic profile—till a DNA profile collected during the raid of Samuel O'Shea's mobile home proved to be a match. In other words, it was O'Shea's DNA that was on the garbage can top, tying him to the firearm..."

Once that had sunk in, Ursula came forward and Declan handed her the stylus, after which she brought up a firearm on the screen and said calmly, "The search of Samuel O'Shea's residence resulted in some interesting finds—including a stockpile of weapons and ammo. Among the firearms seized was the Taurus GX4 9 mm Luger pistol with a suppressor that you see on the monitor. We handed it, along with the ammo collected, over to the forensic science lab. They compared this to the bullets and spent shell casings shot through a Taurus GX4 pistol's gun barrel with five lands and grooves and a left-hand twist used in the murders of Michelle Hewlett and Trevor LeBlanc—and it was a perfect match." She drew a breath. "It was the handgun that was used in the double homicide—with O'Shea pulling the trigger..."

Declan gave a few more remarks afterward, finishing in a confident voice. "The walls are now closing in on Samuel Lochlyn O'Shea. Though he remains at large, all roads out of Bends Lake are being surveilled, and he's effectively boxed in. This doesn't mean he isn't still a serious threat. O'Shea is believed to be armed and dangerous. Not to mention desperate enough that he's as much unpredictable as he had been predictable in his deviant pattern of behavior. That makes him all the more a wild card as we search to find and end the serial killer's reign of murder and mayhem..."

When she was asked to give a closing assessment of Samuel O'Shea, Stella was more than willing to do her part in putting forth a sense of the mindset of O'Shea. Or at the very least, interpreting his calculus for avoiding capture while managing to stay active to feed his homicidal tendencies.

She only wished that Gayle hadn't been a party to her cousin's willingness to become a serial killer—right under her nose. Stella understood, though, that most such skillful killers had a facade, by design. They were able to pull the wool over the unsuspecting eyes of those they purported to be closest to. Why should this time be any different? O'Shea was obviously more than content—not to mention indifferent to how this would impact Gayle in the long run—to exploit her kinship to appear normal himself, while being anything but in his pattern of behavior. It would ultimately take courage and strength by Gayle to overcome Lochlyn's ultimate betrayal and move on with her life as best as possible.

Stella inhaled softly and, after gazing at Declan's handsome face and seeing a twinkle of affection in his eyes, said to the team, "Samuel O'Shea's been exposed for the serial killer he has become. For the better part of his serial killing, he's been totally in his element, living like the cat that ate the canary. But now that he can no longer hide behind the cloak of anonymity and the satisfaction of having a leg up on the rest of us, he is likely calculating his next move to keep his freedom. At the same time, deep down inside, in the vein of the majority of serial killers—O'Shea had to know that his days as a killing machine were not unlimited. By no means, though, does that mean he is ready to throw in the towel. Out of desperation, O'Shea will likely try to find a way to escape the dragnet, even against the odds. That makes him a ticking time bomb that could explode with more killings or other aberrant behavior—if not defused through an arrest or otherwise prevented from doing more harm to others…"

She looked at Declan again and carried on thoughtfully, "I should add that, as with most serial killers, O'Shea could surrender if cornered with no way out. Or he might well go out in a blaze of glory—figuring he's better off dead than spending the rest of his life behind bars. It'll be his call." *Though O'Shea's pursuers might have some say in the matter*, Stella told herself, if there was another way that wouldn't put others at risk. Still, she was well aware of the value in keeping him alive to learn from as a criminal profiler.

"I couldn't agree more with you on how this could end," Declan told her as they started to disband. "I can't get inside O'Shea's head, as you probably can, but there's a third option for bringing this to a conclusion. And that's taking the decision-making out of O'Shea's hands."

"Hmm…" Stella lifted a brow. "You mean capturing him by surprise, before he could react, one way or another?"

Declan gave a thin smile. "Exactly. That is, getting the jump on him with such force and determination that he doesn't know what hit him. Not till it's too late. Hopefully, this would result in O'Shea being taken into custody alive, so that he lives a very, very long time in prison, where he belongs."

"That would certainly be the best-case scenario," she said, nodding. "First, we need to find him and go from there."

"Yeah," Declan concurred. "That shouldn't take much longer. Now that we're onto him, there are only so many places he can duck and hide."

Stella felt the same way. But that still represented quite a few nooks and crannies for O'Shea to try and skirt the law in. In her thinking, this was still one too many when dealing with a cold and calculated serial killer.

DECLAN WAS SITTING in a booth across from Stella at the Bends Lake Coffee House on Rocklear Street, sipping on a breve coffee as his mind wandered between the imminent arrest of Samuel O'Shea and forging ahead with what he hoped would be a love for the ages. He wanted the latter more than anything, though the former carried a lot of weight too, in terms of getting it—the serial killer headache—off their backs, once and for all.

Stella, who was drinking a red-eye coffee, broke his reverie when she asked, ill at ease, "Do you think Gayle could be in danger, as long as O'Shea remains at large?"

Declan jutted his chin musingly. "Doesn't seem like he would go after her, as someone he appears to care for. Beyond that, being on the run while the authorities try to close in on him doesn't exactly leave O'Shea with much wiggle room to target Gayle, whatever his reason might be." Declan tasted the coffee. "Of course, I could be wrong. It's possible that O'Shea could turn on the one person who had his back. At least till she discovered his dark side."

Stella narrowed her eyes and said, "I think I should go talk to her."

Declan raised a brow. "You really think that's a good idea?"

"I know we don't know each other all that well, and I can only imagine what she may be going through at the moment—but having connected at all again, I kind of feel I should reach out to Gayle and offer my support as a friend, as opposed to an FBI special agent." Stella sipped the espresso. "At the very least, I could warn her to be on guard, just to be on the safe side."

"Good idea," Declan said, though they were already keeping tabs on Gayle Reese's workplace and residence, in case O'Shea tried to contact her out of desperation. Right now, though, Declan was more concerned for Stella's health and security. He didn't want to see her end up falling into a serial killer's crosshairs, even if she was more than capable of defending herself as a member of the Bureau. But trying to keep her out of harm's way for personal reasons was probably not the way to go. Not when Stella seemed determined to be there for her high school chum—which was the type of consideration and loyalty that endeared Declan to her, among other qualities she possessed. He eyed her over his mug. "I'm sure Gayle will appreciate you being there for her, under the circumstances."

"She should," Stella concurred. "But honestly, I'm probably thinking just as much about myself and how important it is to have someone there when dealing with a break in family bonding."

"I understand," Declan told her, sitting back. *All too well*, he thought, knowing he hadn't been entirely in Stella's corner as much as he should have when Elise passed away. At the time, he was too caught up in his own grief to lean enough into hers. It was a major regret, and he only wished he could turn back the clock. The good news was that they now had an opportunity to move the clock forward, where he hoped to more than make up for lost time.

STELLA HAD NO qualms returning to the hotel where she'd first stayed when coming back to Bends Lake to work on a serial killer case. At the time, she'd wanted to have as little to do with Declan as possible. Certainly not on an intimate level. But this had all changed. Now she wanted to have everything to do with him as a man who had stolen her heart, body and soul.

As it related to Gayle, Stella wasn't quite sure if she would be welcomed back or not. Neither of them could have expected that Gayle's cousin Lochlyn would become the central character in a serial killer investigation that had brought multiple law enforcement agencies together with one common goal. That being to stop the fatal shootings and hold the person responsible fully accountable.

It seemed to Stella that Gayle felt the same way, recalling her words to that effect: *If Lochlyn is guilty, he needs to answer for it.*

And he will have to at that, Stella told herself with conviction as she watched Gayle approach her in the hotel lobby.

"Hey," Stella said equably.

"Hey." Gayle's eyes were red, as though she had been crying. "I'm glad you wanted to see me. I wanted to see you too."

They sat on plush dark red accent chairs angled toward one another, after which Stella asked sympathetically, "Are you all right?"

Gayle's voice cracked when she answered, "As much as one could be after learning that a cousin who you thought you knew was apparently someone you didn't really know at all. At least not in ways that I could ever have imagined…"

"That could happen to any of us," Stella pointed out. "None of us can read the minds of people who choose to keep their darkest thoughts to themselves."

"I suppose." Gayle shifted her body uncomfortably. "But it still hurts."

"I know." Stella regarded her for a moment or two, thoughtfully. "I have to ask—has Lochlyn tried to contact you?"

"No," she replied without delay. "And I wouldn't want him to, as I'm not sure what I would say to him. Or, for that matter, what he could possibly say to me to justify the truly awful things he's being accused of doing."

"All right." Stella was relieved to know that O'Shea had at least accorded Gayle that much respect in not drawing her any further into his web of terror than he already had. If only by association and bloodline. Even so, desperation could still call for desperate measures from the wanted serial killer. "If by chance Lochlyn does try to reach out to you, Gayle, you need to let me know, and I'll do everything in my power to have this end peacefully—with Lochlyn turning himself in." She realized this was easier said than done, as O'Shea appeared bent on remaining on the loose—while continuing to be a viable threat to anyone whom he might come into contact with.

"I will." Gayle leaned forward to place her hand on Stella's. "Thank you."

Stella nodded. She wanted to say it was her job to run interference. But it went beyond that in this instance. Gayle deserved to see this through with the least amount of damage for her to digest. Just as Declan once did when he lost his first true love—before the time would come to be given another chance at it, which was something Stella embraced with equal optimism.

LOCHLYN WAS WEARING a Kansas City Royals baseball cap tilted low on his forehead, making it harder to identify him. He kept a low profile while on the run from the law after they raided his house, confiscating most of his firearms, and put out a warrant for his arrest. He was angered at the thought, while watching from afar as his cousin Gayle was talking to her friend from high school, Stella.

Having been intrigued by her as someone who reminded him of his ex-wife, he'd coaxed out of Gayle that Stella was an FBI special agent and criminal profiler. Only after he had put two and two together did Lochlyn realize that he had seen the attractive Stella before. It was at Hedy's Club, where she was sitting with, he suspected, other law enforcement personnel. He imagined that they were probably discussing the Bends Lake Predator case.

His own alter ego.

He homed in on Stella chatting with Gayle. *Just what are you saying to my cuz?* Lochlyn asked himself, nostrils flaring. Or vice versa. Was the FBI agent trying to turn his cousin against him?

Lochlyn sucked in a deep breath, controlling his anger, while realizing he couldn't risk being made by any law enforcement who might be lurking around and allowing his presence to be known by either of the women. He had to get out of there without drawing any undue attention.

He peered at Stella once more and told himself, *You and your colleagues may think you've won the battle, but don't get too comfortable in that belief. This isn't over. Trust me.*

We'll see each other again, Special Agent Stella Bailey, Lochlyn promised, but on his own terms. Not hers. Or those of the other law enforcement personnel who wanted to take him down then gloat about it afterward, patting themselves on the back. But he wasn't about to go down easily. It wasn't in his DNA. He was not quite through with his self-proclaimed mission of elimination.

He took one last look at the special agent and his cousin, then quietly found a side exit and slithered out of the hotel unscathed, while deep dark thoughts circulated in his mind with pleasure and promise as he walked away.

Chapter Sixteen

A license plate reader picked up the black Cadillac Escalade SUV that was registered to Samuel L. O'Shea cruising down Brownstin Lane, not far from the Nineteenth Street intersection. As a squad car trailed the suspect's vehicle, Declan converged on the scene in his Chevrolet Malibu, along with other law enforcement. They were all on the same page in wanting to stop the suspect in his tracks, once and for all.

Only then can we all breathe a collective sigh of relief in getting a stone-cold killer off the streets, Declan told himself, as he reached Nineteenth Street ahead of the Escalade, where a blockade had already been put in place to stop oncoming traffic and prevent the suspect from advancing farther.

Exiting his own vehicle, Declan met up with Stella, who came with Arielle and other law enforcement, including sharpshooters. Everyone wore ballistic vests, not knowing how this thing might end, but prepared for O'Shea to engage in a gunfight rather than be taken in alive.

"You ready for this?" Declan asked Stella, though knowing the answer.

"I think we all are," she told him matter-of-factly.

"Let's just get it over with—hopefully with O'Shea laying down his firearm peacefully."

"Wouldn't that be nice?" Arielle chipped in, not sounding too optimistic.

"Yeah." Declan kept his mind open either way, as he spoke to the SWAT team commander Jay Yonamine, a hulking fortysomething man with a short brown military haircut. "Let's do this."

Jay nodded, eyed others in place and ready for whatever came their way, then declared, "It's game time!"

Game time it is, Declan told himself, as he turned to see the suspect's SUV approaching.

It was quickly surrounded by law enforcement vehicles, shielding armed personnel, including Declan and Stella.

"KBI. Get out of the vehicle—slowly and with your hands up!" Declan ordered the suspect. "Now!"

The suspect appeared startled, but obeyed, opening the door and stepping outside carefully. He put his hands atop his head, as though he'd been through this scenario before.

"Don't move!" Jay's voice boomed from behind an FBI van.

Declan peered at the suspect, studying him as though a specimen in a laboratory. He was white and looked to be in his midtwenties, tall and lanky, with blond hair in a half-up ponytail and a brunette chin strap beard.

"It's not O'Shea," Stella said, a catch to her voice.

"No kidding," Declan responded sardonically, while in complete agreement. Yet it was definitely the suspect's SUV. "So where the hell is Samuel L. O'Shea? And why is this man driving his Cadillac Escalade?"

"Good question," she uttered.

They wasted little time in seeking answers, as the SUV driver was ordered onto his knees before it was deemed safe enough for law enforcement to rush him. He was checked for weapons—and found to be unarmed—pulled to his feet and handcuffed behind his back.

Only then did Declan put his SIG Sauer firearm back in its holster and approach the man. "I'm Special Agent Delgado. Who are you?"

The man blinked blue eyes and responded, "Martin Poole."

Declan favored him with a hard stare. "What are you doing with this vehicle?"

Poole hunched a shoulder flippantly. "Uh, driving it."

"I can see that," Declan said tersely. "Question is why?" He considered whether this was a ploy by O'Shea to buy himself some time. "Did Samuel O'Shea, the owner of the SUV, put you up to this to send us on a wild-goose chase?"

"I don't know anything about that," Poole claimed, seemingly beating around the bush.

"What do you know?" Declan glared at him. "This isn't a game. The man the Cadillac Escalade is registered to is wanted for murder. If you're an accomplice—"

"I'm not." Poole licked his lips nervously. "Look, I stole the SUV, okay? I saw a man ditch it and run off, as if wanting to have nothing more to do with it. I checked it out and saw the key was left in the ignition. I needed a ride, so I took it. That's all."

Declan regarded him dubiously and said, "Describe the man who ditched the Escalade—"

Poole described Samuel O'Shea to a T. Though there

was still reason to believe Poole's story could be made up, it was just as plausible that he was telling the truth. Declan watched as Arielle came up and asked Poole, "Did you see him get into another vehicle?"

Poole shook his head. "No, he just ran down the street."

Declan asked, "What street was that?"

Poole replied anxiously, "Trowridge Avenue, a few blocks from Brownstin Lane."

Not too far away, Declan thought. But far enough to give O'Shea some latitude to seek other transportation to remain on the lamb.

"Take him away," Declan said, scowling at Martin Poole, who, at the very least, would be charged with auto theft. Even if he happened to have stolen a vehicle that belonged to the Bends Lake Predator, who had managed to outsmart them again.

Declan saw this as only a short-term victory for O'Shea, while conceding that short was relative. Meaning that it still gave the suspect enough time to cause more trouble—if they didn't catch up to him soon. But at least they had O'Shea's SUV in their possession, which would undoubtedly provide more evidence to tie him to the vehicle and, by association, the homicides the suspect was believed to have committed.

LOCHLYN WAS ONLY too happy to have outsmarted the authorities. Once he knew that they had latched on to his Cadillac Escalade, rather than switch the license plates but risk being stopped anyway, he chose to unload the SUV instead and find another vehicle to drive and in which to make his escape.

The fact that he spotted, while hidden in a wooded area, the Escalade being driven by someone looking for a free ride, played right into his hands. Lochlyn would use the subterfuge of pointing the KBI in the wrong direction to stay one step ahead of them, while continuing his deadly agenda as the Bends Lake Predator.

After which he would find a way to get out of Dodge, so to speak, and seek greener pastures to resume killing as he saw fit.

Lochlyn was on the move, his eyes darting this way and that to keep abreast of his surroundings and any signs that the authorities were onto him. He wished he could say goodbye to Gayle as the one person who seemed to give a damn about him. But circumstances stood in the way. That certainly wasn't true where it concerned his ex-wife. And definitely not Diane Wexler, who wouldn't give him the time of day and paid the price. Not even his last employer, who gave him the boot unjustly, leaving him high and dry.

But who needed any of them? He was always one to carve his own path. Why should this be any different? Why would he want it to be, when he always landed on his feet at the end of the day?

Lochlyn spied a bald-headed elderly man in front of a home on Youngston Street. He was about to enter a white Lincoln Navigator Reserve.

Perfect for me, Lochlyn thought, grinning as he took a black Wilson Combat SFX9 9 mm Luger handgun that had a silencer out of his jacket pocket. He moved briskly toward the man before he could enter the car.

Sticking the gun into the old man's shocked face, Lochlyn said simply, "We can either do this the easy way or the hard way." Then he grinned as the man seemed to be considering his options and told him with a sardonic chuckle, "Actually, I think I like the easy way for me and the hard way for you..."

Lochlyn pulled the trigger, hitting the man in the head twice in rapid-fire action, watching unemotionally as he fell down like a collapsed building.

Too bad, so sad, Lochlyn thought heartlessly, as he took the dead man's keys and claimed the car as his own before getting behind the wheel, starting it and driving off, while leaving behind another victim.

AFTER RECEIVING THE call about a fatal carjacking on Youngston Street, Ursula went to the scene, alongside Special Agent Noah Rudd, who drove. Both were suspicious about the timing of the crime, which coincided with the hunt for Samuel O'Shea, who had ditched his Cadillac Escalade and was on the run.

Ursula was still smarting that O'Shea had outmaneuvered them yet again in his latest move to dodge accountability for his lethal criminality. They had to put a stop to his lunacy, once and for all. But had the serial killer struck again in the meantime?

When they arrived at the scene, both special agents rendezvoused with the first responder, Bends Lake Police Officer Jeremy Ponte, who said bleakly, "We've got an eighty-one-year-old dead male, identified as Sheldon Ferreira. He was apparently about to enter his vehicle, when the carjacker took him by surprise."

Ursula eyed the frail victim, who was lying face down in his own blood, two bullet wounds visible in the back of his head. She spotted the spent shell casings near the curb and wondered if the man had tried to put up a fight for his life—possibly triggering the shooting. Or had he thought it was a losing cause and succumbed to the fateful moment at hand?

Noah regarded the victim and, furrowing his brow, commented, "Looks like an execution-style killing."

Jeremy said, "I was thinking the same thing. I have a feeling the victim didn't necessarily know what was coming, but still found himself on the wrong end of a gun and helpless to defend himself."

"Any witnesses?" Ursula asked him.

"Yeah." Jeremy jutted his chin. "A 911 call reported a man driving off in the victim's white Lincoln Navigator Reserve."

"Hmm," Noah muttered thoughtfully. "We'll get the license plate number and put out a BOLO alert for the vehicle and driver."

Ursula looked around. "I'm guessing that some of the homes on this block and nearby have surveillance cameras that may have caught the unsub on foot prior to the carjacking—or afterward when driving off with the stolen vehicle."

"We're checking that out," Jeremy told her.

"Good." Ursula took out her cell phone and contacted Declan, knowing that they were possibly dealing with another murder courtesy of Samuel O'Shea.

Declan told her bluntly, "At this point, I wouldn't put it past O'Shea to go after anyone who got in his way or had something he desperately needed—like another means of transportation."

"Neither would I," she admitted. "We'll see if we can make the connection to O'Shea."

After they ended the call, Ursula and Noah did some door-to-door interviews before the medical examiner and Crime Scene Response Team arrived to perform their respective duties on the latest homicide to hit Bends Lake.

INSIDE HIS HOME OFFICE, Declan and Stella were standing at the workstation, reviewing surveillance footage that showed a man who closely resembled Samuel O'Shea driving the Lincoln Navigator Reserve registered to Sheldon Ferreira, a widower, who had been shot to death by the carjacker.

"It's him," Declan stated with near certainty. "O'Shea is stooping to the lowest depths in his penchant for violence and escaping justice."

Stella, gazing at the laptop in front of them, said, "Not surprising, really. It's almost like now that the curtain of anonymity has been pulled back, he feels emboldened enough to own up to shooting people in broad daylight. He's pretty much daring us to catch him if we can."

It was a dare that spoke to Declan. He took it personally, within the context of a KBI special agent, wanting to be the one to slap the cuffs on the serial killer, if possible. "We're more than happy to oblige," Declan said, an edge to his voice. "We know what O'Shea is driving, and there's no escaping Bends Lake—so the clock's ticking, and his time is definitely running out."

"Seems to be the case," she concurred. "Problem is, until such time, who else will be dragged into his horror show—and maybe never again see the light of day…?"

It was a question that Declan asked himself, more than once, disliking the answer more the longer this thing went on. He could only be optimistic in replying, "No one if we're lucky."

She cocked a brow. "And if we aren't?"

He swallowed, touching her soft hand. "Then O'Shea could still set his sights on others, with all bets off on the outcome—"

But Declan refused to go there, with his gut telling him that this was about to come to a head, one way or the other.

Stella looked at him and switched the subject, as she said, "I thought we could do takeout for dinner this evening."

"What did you have in mind?" He was amenable to taking a break from making each other meals—even if he never tired of feeding her and watching as she ate, whenever the opportunity arose.

"I have a taste for Chinese food. Harry's Wok House isn't far from here."

Declan told her, "I know the place. Been there once or twice."

She nodded and said, "I can order and we'll pick it up—along with a bottle of wine."

He smiled and imagined tasting the wine on her lips with a kiss. "Sounds good to me."

"Okay." Stella gazed at him and took out her cell phone.

Declan turned back to his laptop, where he had a video chat request from Josephine Okamura. After accepting it, he gazed at her and said, "Hey."

She smiled, touching her glasses. "I wanted to let you know that we were able to analyze the bullets that killed

Sheldon Ferreira and the spent shell casings found at the crime scene…"

He peered at her. "All right."

Josephine stated evenly, "Aside from being a match, they came from a Wilson Combat SFX9 9 mm Luger pistol—and were shot through a gun barrel with five lands and grooves and a right-hand twist."

"Hmm…" Declan mused about the latest firearm that was used by Samuel O'Shea to carry out his homicides. A search of his Cadillac Escalade had come up empty insofar as he hadn't left behind any weapons after dumping the SUV as part of his effort to evade capture. But O'Shea's DNA and prints were present throughout the Escalade, tying it directly to him and the serial murders he perpetrated while using the vehicle to come and go from crime scenes. "I'll make a note of your findings on the handgun, Josephine, as we piece together our case against the suspect."

"Thanks." She smiled. "Happy to do my part here."

Declan nodded and ended the chat. He saw that Stella was off the phone and said to her, "Are we all set for some Chinese takeout?"

"Yes." Stella grinned. "Hope you're hungry?"

"I am." Declan moved up to her. "Especially for this…" He cupped her cheeks and gave Stella a nice long kiss.

"Umm…" she cooed, touching her lips. "I meant food."

"Yeah, that too." He laughed. "Let's go pick up our dinner."

AFTER DECLAN DROVE into the parking lot of the strip mall on Lewellen Drive and parked, they got out of the car and he said, "While you're grabbing the food, I'll head over to the store and get the wine."

"Sounds good," Stella said, eyeing the Bends Lake Mini Mart, two places down from Harry's Wok House. "I'll meet you outside."

"Okay." Declan caressed her cheek, sending electrical sparks throughout Stella's body, as was often the case when he touched her.

They separated and she went inside the Chinese restaurant, where she picked up the order of vegetable spring rolls and fried chicken wings.

While paying, Stella hardly noticed the man wearing a hoodie who entered the place and moved in her direction. Only when she caught sight of him in her periphery did she turn his way. It took Stella only an instant to recognize Gayle's cousin Lochlyn, aka Samuel L. O'Shea.

His countenance dark with deviance, Lochlyn said menacingly, "Nice to see you again, Stella." He laughed crudely. "Or maybe not so much—for you, anyway..."

Stella was just about to offer a sarcastic comeback for the serial killer suspect, but held her tongue when she saw him remove from his pocket the Wilson Combat SFX9 9 mm Luger pistol that Declan had alluded to during the drive that O'Shea had used to commit murder during the carjacking.

She managed to control her emotions as Stella said coolly, "You don't have to do this, Lochlyn."

He chuckled and snorted, "I'm afraid I do, Special Agent Bailey. After poisoning Gayle against me, you've left me little choice. Now, let's walk out of here together, so I don't have to shoot both you and that pretty young thing at the counter for the bargain—"

"All right." Stella got the message, loud and clear. She certainly had no wish to see anyone else hurt by this monster. That included herself. But she knew that all bets were off, so long as he held a gun to her chest, having already shown a willingness to pull the trigger, time and time again.

At gunpoint, Stella led the way as she and her accoster exited the restaurant, not knowing if she would ever see Declan again, to tell him how much she loved and felt loved by him.

Chapter Seventeen

Declan had just paid for a bottle of Cabernet Sauvignon and was leaving the checkout counter when his cell phone rang. He pulled it out and saw that the caller was Ursula then answered equably, "Hey."

"The Lincoln Navigator Reserve stolen by Samuel O'Shea was spotted by an automated license plate reader surveillance camera on Lewellen Drive," she told him. "It looked to be headed for the Mackton Center strip mall..."

"What?" Declan reacted as a sense of dread swept over him like an ominous shroud. His heart skipped a beat as he uttered, "I happen to be there right now, at a store. Worse is that Stella's here too, inside a Chinese restaurant picking up an order."

Ursula sighed into the phone. "You don't think O'Shea is coming after her—?"

"I sure as hell hope not," Declan responded, but his pulse quickened as he told himself instinctively, *I honestly can't rule that out. Can I?* "But it's entirely possible," he had to admit. "Maybe O'Shea somehow tracked Stella and feels he has a score to settle now that he was ratted out by his cousin Gayle Reese—with Stella the common denominator."

"That doesn't sound good." Ursula groaned. "We're

zeroing in on the location even as we speak—and we'll take O'Shea down." She paused. "Go get Stella."

"Yeah, I will." Declan sucked in a deep breath as he headed out of the store as though his life depended on it. In actuality, it was Stella's life that was in jeopardy. The mere thought of losing someone else he was in love with made him weak in the knees. Or worse, totally heartbroken. He couldn't bear not being able to have the type of relationship with Stella that they had both deprived themselves of experiencing the first time around.

I owe it to you, Stella, to make things right, once and for all, Declan told himself as he left the store. He was glad that he had instinctively brought along his SIG Sauer P226 pistol. Unfortunately, Stella had not armed herself with her Glock 19 9x19 mm handgun. She had trusted him to protect them both. *I can't let her down—my love*, he thought, with fierce determination, even as Declan had a dreadful feeling that he might have already been too late to act.

Why didn't I bring my pistol? Stella asked herself, in a classic case of second-guessing when the chips were down, as was the case in her current predicament. Too late now. She had little choice but to deal with the situation as it was—knowing that Samuel O'Shea fully intended to kill her, if he got his way, much like the others whose lives he ended by gunfire.

After he had used his free hand to unnecessarily frisk her for weapons, seeing that her form-fitting knit top and straight leg jeans left little room for a concealed firearm, O'Shea said smugly, "Had to check. Wouldn't have wanted you to catch me napping by whipping out your gun from somewhere and actually shooting me with it." He laughed mirthlessly.

They had moved away from the Chinese restaurant, and Stella had dropped her takeout order, figuring that food was the least of her concerns right now. She suspected that Declan may have left the store and was privy to what was going on. But what if that wasn't the case? Would it be too little, too late for him to intervene?

"Where are we going?" Stella asked her assailant, if only to buy time and contemplate how she might be able to gain the upper hand.

"Away from here—and KBI special agent Delgado," O'Shea said arrogantly, holding the Wilson Combat SFX9 9 mm Luger pistol fitted with a silencer to her back. "I followed you from the hotel after I saw you talking to Gayle—and to a house with Delgado there. It wasn't difficult putting two and two together. Just needed an opportunity to separate you from the special agent— to make you pay for sticking your nose where it wasn't wanted…before getting out of Bends Lake for good."

Stella could see that they were headed toward the Lincoln Navigator that O'Shea had carjacked, which was parked at the far end of the Mini Mart. She looked at the culprit over her shoulder and, recalling his accusation that she had poisoned Gayle against him, uttered pointedly, "Just for the record, I never stuck my nose anywhere. Whatever issues you have with Gayle, you have no one to blame but yourself. As far as her cooperation, she really had no choice, since you were wanted on suspicion of numerous murders. So why not just give up, Lochlyn—instead of only compounding your troubles by killing me?"

Stella doubted she would be able to reach any degree of compunction inside him as a serial killer bent on carrying out his maniacal agenda, but hoped—if nothing else—to rattle him just a little. Especially as she sensed that they were being watched and something was about to go down that could mean the end of her life...or the beginning of a future.

O'Shea laughed sardonically. "Oh, you'd like that, wouldn't you? Sorry, not going to happen. I'm not about to throw in the towel. I'm having too much fun running rings around the KBI, FBI, PD, you name it." They reached the stolen vehicle, and he opened the passenger door. Aiming the gun at her, he gave her a once-over and said musingly, "By the way, you remind me so much of my ex-wife... Should've killed her when I had the chance." His forehead furrowed. "Oh well... Looks like I've found the perfect substitute—in you..."

Stella swallowed thickly while assessing his illogical perspective. "Taking my life will never make up for letting your ex-wife off the hook," she argued, doubting it would make any difference at this point.

"We'll see about that," he hissed, then ordered with a sneer, "Get in, Agent Bailey. We're going for a little drive to put some distance between here and your boyfriend—otherwise, I'll have to shoot you right here and now and be done with it..."

"Okay, you win," Stella pretended to give in. "I'll do whatever you say." She furrowed her brow at him. "Isn't that what you've come to expect from all your victims before shooting them to death? To totally submit to your will and their fate?"

O'Shea chuckled. "Yeah, that's about the size of it.

Never fails." He laughed again and stopped on a dime. "Inside..." He pointed at the passenger seat.

Just then, they both heard a noise, causing O'Shea to look away from her for just an instant. *It's now or possibly never*, Stella told herself. Swiftly grabbing the wrist of his gun hand, she twisted the barrel away from her face—then turned to a karate self-defense technique she had learned. With her fist, she hit him with a *choku zuki*—or straight punch—in the face, as hard as she could. She quickly followed with a *mawashi zuki*—which was a round hook punch—to the jaw and then gave him a *hiza geri*, or knee kick to the groin.

Her quick moves caught him off guard as O'Shea howled in pain and fury, while trying to regain control of his gun hand. As Stella fought to stay alive, Declan appeared seemingly out of nowhere and twisted O'Shea's wrist in a way that forced the Wilson Combat SFX9 handgun out of his hand, falling to the ground. But not before O'Shea managed to get off a shot that went harmlessly into the air.

Afterward, Declan hit him with a hard uppercut to the chin and another blow to the right cheek before stepping aside as a wobbly O'Shea was summarily surrounded by heavily armed law enforcement, who overcame his feeble efforts to resist, taking him into custody.

Ursula, putting her firearm back in its holster, gazed at Stella and asked, concern in her tone, "Are you all right?"

"Yes, thank goodness." Stella smiled at her. "A little unnerved but otherwise unharmed."

"Great." Ursula regarded Declan. "The system worked."

"Yeah, it did," he acknowledged, giving her an appreciative nod.

As Ursula stepped away, Stella hugged Declan shamelessly. "Thanks for coming to my rescue," she uttered softly.

"Believe me, I didn't have any other choice," he spoke matter-of-factly. "I wasn't about to let O'Shea claim another victim—least of all you."

"That's nice to know," Stella cooed. "The thought that this could have turned out very differently—" She choked back the words.

"It didn't." Declan touched her cheek. "Neither of us were ready for this—us—to end. Not in that way."

Stella grinned knowingly. "No, we weren't."

"Have to say, you did a great job in getting O'Shea's attention." Declan gave a laugh. "You put some moves on him that took away any perceived advantage he thought he had."

She chuckled. "Karate is always a nice go-to when all else fails."

"No arguing with that." He took her hand and said cheerfully, "Why don't we go and reorder that Chinese meal, so we'll have something tasty to eat with the wine I purchased."

She chuckled. "Sounds like a good idea to me."

THE FOLLOWING DAY, after giving Samuel Lochlyn O'Shea a night to mull over just what he'd done and would have to answer for, Declan sat across from the captured Bends Lake Predator suspect in an interrogation room at the Danver County Detention Facility on Krepton Road. O'Shea was wearing an orange jail jumpsuit and shackles. He winced, no doubt still smarting from Stella's impressive karate self-defense and Declan eagerly coming to her aide after the suspect's attempt to kidnap her and worse.

Quite frankly, Declan wasn't sure what they would get out of the purported serial killer—him having been read his rights against self-incrimination—but they wanted him on the official record for whatever he wished to say. That, however, would likely be limited, as O'Shea sat next to his court-appointed attorney named Loralee Santana, who was fortysomething with blond hair in an A-line bob cut and wore oval eyeglasses.

Declan mused about Stella watching the interrogation on a video monitor in her capacity as an FBI behavioral analyst—as opposed to a damned near murder victim—in assessing O'Shea's state of mind as the case against him moved forward.

Peering at the suspect, Declan said sharply, "The Wilson Combat SFX9 handgun you were carrying has been positively linked to the bullets and shell casings left behind in the murder of Sheldon Ferreira. We also have your DNA and prints taken from Ferreira's Lincoln Navigator Reserve that you carjacked. How's that for starters?"

O'Shea shrugged dismissively. "So, tell me something I don't already know."

Declan set his jaw. "Well, since you mention it, here's something you probably weren't aware of... A new witness has come forward with video that places you directly at the scene of the murder of Peggy Elizondo in Blakely Park," he decided to share with the suspect. In fact, the witness, a professional photographer by the name of Ulysses Espelita, had taken the video randomly and from a distance and only recently reviewed it, making his shocking discovery.

Loralee looked at her client. "You're not obligated to respond to this allegation," she cautioned.

O'Shea rolled his eyes. "Whatever."

Declan pushed forward, sensing an opening till proven otherwise. He asked the suspect point-blank, "Maybe you'd like to get off your chest what motivated you to shoot to death ten different people—male and female—with the full intention of killing two others?"

Loralee again intervened. "I would recommend you not answer that."

O'Shea leaned toward his attorney and whispered in her ear. Loralee whispered back, before O'Shea glared at Declan and responded glibly, "Do I need a reason?"

"You tell me." Declan's chin jutted. "What would possess you to become a serial killer?" He was sure there was some method to his madness, whether the suspect cared to divulge this or not.

O'Shea licked his lips and responded boastfully, "The same thing as other serial killers. I needed to take out my frustrations, for this reason or that, and found some ready-made targets to go after in giving me the release I needed. What can I say?"

"I don't think you should say anything else," Loralee told him, her agitation evident.

Declan gave him an out by stating, "We can stop this anytime you like."

O'Shea cracked a grin. "If I had my way, it would never have stopped. Why would I, if you people were too inept to stop me from killing?"

I don't doubt for one minute that he had every inten-

tion of continuing the murders indefinitely, if allowed to, Declan told himself. He watched as the suspect's lawyer looked as though she wanted to tape his mouth shut, but could only sit back and stew while O'Shea dug his own hole and fell deeper into it.

Declan glanced at the video camera and fixed the suspect's smug face as he asked him coolly, "So were most of these ready-made targets, as you called them, randomly chosen? Or was there some personal vendetta against all of them—such as with Diane Wexler?"

Loralee pushed up her glasses and warned her client, "I really advise you to end this—now!"

O'Shea waved her off and said contemptuously, "Diane was the only one I had a score to settle with. The others were simply there to pick off when the mood hit me and opportunity came my way." He narrowed his eyes at Declan. "I have to tell you, though, Special Agent Delgado, I would've truly enjoyed killing Stella if I'd been able to finish the job. Because she messed things up between me and my cousin Gayle—and gave me flashbacks of my ex-wife—Special Agent Bailey deserved to die."

Declan chose to bite his tongue rather than to allow the serial killer to bait him into crossing the line in defense of Stella, while watching as Loralee admonished her client.

She finally snapped, "This interview is over!"

Declan nodded with a deep sigh, having heard all he needed to from Samuel Lochlyn O'Shea to know that he was going down for his many crimes, and there was no way he'd ever see freedom again.

After ending the interrogation, Declan signaled to a guard to escort the suspect back to his cell.

"SAMUEL O'SHEA... LOCHLYN...is the quintessential narcissist," Stella told Declan as they stood on his land gazing at the Cheyenne Bottoms wetland. She was still coming to terms with her attempted abductor and confessed serial killer's interrogation an hour ago, which came to an abrupt halt once his attorney finally got her wish to put a lid on it. But the damage had already been done, as O'Shea's ego simply got the better of him. With just enough encouragement from Declan. "The man's inflated sense of self-worth is right there with the likes of fellow serial killers Ted Bundy and Henry Lee Lucas, among others, who see themselves as super smart and cunning to the point of controlling the narrative, even while behind bars."

Declan bristled. "As long as O'Shea can never again harm any others on the outside, he's free to boast about his homicidal tendencies and dark thoughts in that regard. I'm just glad that he was unsuccessful in making you another fatal victim of his sick penchant for murder..."

"You and me both." Stella grinned at him. She was forever grateful that what they had established with each other had not been cut short through forces beyond their control. "In an odd way, Lochlyn—as despicable as he is—was able to bring us back together, after it seemed as though the window had closed for good."

"You're right about that. Fate, however one chooses to look at it, somehow intervened in bridging the gap between us." Declan regarded her thoughtfully. "I couldn't be happier that it happened."

"Neither could I," Stella made clear, and wondered where they would go from there. If anywhere.

"So...now that the case has been solved for all intents and purposes, I suppose you'll be heading back to Detroit and the life you've built there...?"

She batted her lashes at him. "Is that what you want?"

He paused, putting his hands on her shoulders. "Only if I can come with you."

Stella inhaled quietly, meeting his gaze. "What are you saying?"

Declan peered intensely into her eyes, making Stella feel the heat throughout her body, as he answered deliberately, "I'm saying that I'm in love with you—deeply so—and I want us to make a life together, in Detroit, Bends Lake or anywhere else."

She uttered, "I want that too..." He took her quivering hands, and she felt the steadiness of his calming them.

"Good." Declan flashed her a boyish grin. Suddenly, he dropped to one knee and removed a small box from the pocket of his cashmere blazer. He opened it to reveal a yellow diamond ring. "Stella Meredith Bailey, I'm asking you to become my wife and give us both a second shot at finding the happiness we both deserve. Please say yes and make my dream come true of being the best husband I can for you—and hopefully having the opportunity to be the best father for our children, knowing you'd be the best mother..."

Stella flushed with happiness as she waited a beat to allow the incredible moment to sink in, before gazing into his eyes and crying, "Yes, yes, yes, Declan Scott

Delgado—" she thought it cute to use their middle names in their romance words to each other "—I will definitely marry you, as I love you with all my heart!"

"So happy to hear you say that, Stella!" Declan's face lit up. "Music to my ears."

Stella's teeth shone brightly. "I love the melody too," she cooed, and held out her ring finger with expectation as he removed the ring, with its pavé diamond platinum band, and slid it onto her finger in what was a perfect fit. "Now get up and kiss me, Declan, to make our engagement and future together complete!"

Declan laughed. "With pleasure."

He rose to his feet in leather Chelsea boots, cupped her cheeks and laid a powerful kiss on her generous mouth that quite literally had Stella melting into his arms as Declan wrapped them joyously around her—both undeniably ecstatic about the life, love and family they had to look forward to.

Epilogue

A year later, Stella Delgado sat at the Bends Lake Bookstore on Picktor Drive, signing copies of her hot new book on criminal profiling. It never failed to amaze her how the subject matter seemed to strike a chord with the public as much as criminologists and law enforcement. The fact that this book included a chapter on the infamous Bends Lake Predator, aka Samuel Lochlyn O'Shea, piqued the interest of locals to an even greater degree.

After brazenly confessing to committing ten murders, attempting to murder two others, carjacking, possessing illegal firearms and related charges, O'Shea was sentenced to life behind bars without even the slightest possibility of parole. He would serve out his long days and short nights at the El Dorado Correctional Facility, a maximum-security prison located on State Highway 54, just east of the city of El Dorado in Prospect Township, Butler County, Kansas.

To Stella, O'Shea was getting his just reward for choosing to become a serial killer and showing no remorse, which was par for the course for most serial killers in society. Giving his surviving victims some peace of mind—herself included—made solving the case that much more satisfying.

Stella prepared to sign another copy of the book, already a bestseller. She gazed up at the handsome face of her husband of six months. Declan was, as always, her biggest supporter and the one person she loved spending every moment with. Stella's transfer to the Bureau's Kansas City field office allowed Declan to remain a dedicated KBI special agent, in spite of being more than willing to quit his job. He had, in fact, made serious inquiries about taking a position with the Michigan Department of Attorney General's Criminal Investigations Division.

And she loved him for it. But she knew this was exactly where they belonged. Returning home felt right to Stella, for both the memory of her sister and building a solid foundation to start a family. Her parents were fully supportive, inviting them to Detroit anytime they wished to visit.

"Hey." Declan's smooth voice broke her reverie. "Think I might be able to get a signed copy of your book to cherish, Mrs. Delgado—just as I do its author?"

Stella flashed him a brilliant smile. "Why certainly, Mr. Delgado. It would give me no greater pleasure than to put my autograph on your copy."

"Terrific!" Declan tilted his head. "And I mean that in more ways than one."

Stella took that for everything it was worth, and that was plenty. After she signed the book and finished by writing, *Yours Forever and Ever, Love Stella*, Declan broke into an emotional, slanted grin and uttered without prelude, "Back at you, my darling!"

He punctuated this by leaning over the table and shamelessly giving her a short, but always ever sweet, kiss.

* * * * *

Get up to 4 Free Books!

We'll send you 2 free books from each series you try PLUS a free Mystery Gift.

FREE Value Over **$25**

Both the **Harlequin Intrigue®** and **Harlequin® Romantic Suspense** series feature compelling novels filled with heart-racing action-packed romance that will keep you on the edge of your seat.

YES! Please send me 2 FREE novels from the Harlequin Intrigue or Harlequin Romantic Suspense series and my FREE gift (gift is worth about $10 retail). After receiving them, if I don't wish to receive any more books, I can return the shipping statement marked "cancel." If I don't cancel, I will receive 6 brand-new Harlequin Intrigue Larger-Print books every month and be billed just $7.19 each in the U.S. or $7.99 each in Canada, or 4 brand-new Harlequin Romantic Suspense books every month and be billed just $6.39 each in the U.S. or $7.19 each in Canada, a savings of 20% off the cover price. It's quite a bargain! Shipping and handling is just 50¢ per book in the U.S. and $1.25 per book in Canada.* I understand that accepting the 2 free books and gift places me under no obligation to buy anything. I can always return a shipment and cancel at any time by calling the number below. The free books and gift are mine to keep no matter what I decide.

Choose one:
- ☐ **Harlequin Intrigue Larger-Print** (199/399 BPA G36Y)
- ☐ **Harlequin Romantic Suspense** (240/340 BPA G36Y)
- ☐ **Or Try Both!** (199/399 & 240/340 BPA G36Z)

Name (please print)

Address   Apt. #

City   State/Province   Zip/Postal Code

Email: Please check this box ☐ if you would like to receive newsletters and promotional emails from Harlequin Enterprises ULC and its affiliates. You can unsubscribe anytime.

Mail to the Harlequin Reader Service:
IN U.S.A.: P.O. Box 1341, Buffalo, NY 14240-8531
IN CANADA: P.O. Box 603, Fort Erie, Ontario L2A 5X3

Want to explore our other series or interested in ebooks? Visit **www.ReaderService.com** or call 1-800-873-8635.

---

*Terms and prices subject to change without notice. Prices do not include sales taxes, which will be charged (if applicable) based on your state or country of residence. Canadian residents will be charged applicable taxes. Offer not valid in Quebec. This offer is limited to one order per household. Books received may not be as shown. Not valid for current subscribers to the Harlequin Intrigue or Harlequin Romantic Suspense series. All orders subject to approval. Credit or debit balances in a customer's account(s) may be offset by any other outstanding balance owed by or to the customer. Please allow 4 to 6 weeks for delivery. Offer available while quantities last.

Your Privacy—Your information is being collected by Harlequin Enterprises ULC, operating as Harlequin Reader Service. For a complete summary of the information we collect, how we use this information and to whom it is disclosed, please visit our privacy notice located at https://corporate.harlequin.com/privacy-notice. Notice to California Residents – Under California law, you have specific rights to control and access your data. For more information on these rights and how to exercise them, visit https://corporate.harlequin.com/california-privacy. For additional information for residents of other U.S. states that provide their residents with certain rights with respect to personal data, visit https://corporate.harlequin.com/other-state-residents-privacy-rights/.